seduced
by the
soldier

seduced
by the
soldier

MELIA ALEXANDER

Entangled Publishing, LLC
2614 South Timberline Road
Suite 105, PMB 159
Fort Collins, CO 80525
rights@entangledpublishing.com

Lovestruck is an imprint of Entangled Publishing, LLC.

Edited by Heather Howland
Cover design by Bree Archer
Cover photography by Master1305/Shutterstock
bbsferrari/Getty Images

Manufactured in the United States of America

First Edition November 2019

To the Chamorro people of Guam, my island home. From you came the legends that fueled my imagination and gifted me with the love of storytelling. Si Yu'us Ma'åse! *I am forever grateful.*

Chapter One

Zandra York readjusted her crossbody bag and dragged her roller behind her as she scanned the signs for baggage claim, her nerves a jumble of anxious excitement, jet lag, and the need to get away from her obnoxious seatmate.

Her first international flight hadn't exactly been stellar. How she made it across the Atlantic without smacking the guy was beyond her. He clearly had no filters when it came to flying etiquette. Hell, he probably had few filters at all. Who would help himself to a fellow traveler's leftover food? Who sang—badly—the lyrics to Queen's "Bohemian Rhapsody" in an effort to drown out the sound of the plane's engines?

Unfortunately, her earbuds hadn't been much help. Equally unfortunate was that smacking someone wouldn't help her brand. Nope. The world knew Zandra York as friendly and engaging, not someone who assaulted loud, noisy people when they were all packed tight in a flying tin can. Then again, the other passengers might've appreciated it.

Zandra eased in a deep breath. Calm. She had to stay

calm. She was well on her way to redefining herself. After all, she was morphing into Zandra 2.0, and that meant she knew what she wanted and wasn't afraid to go after it, no matter what anyone else thought. What she lacked in skills or knowledge she'd figure out. She could do this thing called *life*.

Life. Right.

She passed a gift shop and focused on the rack of T-shirts with a heart and *Frankfurt, Germany* emblazoned across them. Hearts. She smiled. Hearts were her talisman, a symbol that everything was going to be fine. She took another deep breath and reached for her cell.

Now would be a good time to slip in a quick livestream. The fact she'd had less than an hour nap on a seven-hour flight? Or that she'd been exhausted from her besties' weekend bachelorette party, Chicago-style?

Who cared? It was all about giving her followers a peek into her life. Never mind that most of them were friends and family who'd turned their Instagram notifications on specifically for this trip, mainly because they wanted to know she'd made it in one piece.

Besides, she wanted to share this moment with them because, hello, she was in freakin' *Germany*.

She grinned. Her. First. Real. Assignment.

A zing of electricity flowed through her, anticipation seeping into every cell. *Flights and Sights* had finally taken a chance with her. They wanted to use her quirky, fun style of photography in their next edition, and she was going to deliver. She could do this, foreign country or not. The e-zine had made it clear: she turned in photos that sold more e-zine subscriptions, and there'd be a much-needed, sizable bonus at the end of this rainbow, along with an even better assignment. Didn't matter where it was, she'd go.

She pulled up Instagram, tapped the icon, and held her cell phone at just the right angle to capture the slight tilt of her head. The guy at the cell phone store swore the card he'd put in would work anywhere in the world, but she still held her breath as she waited for the connection. Zandra blew out a breath when it finally went through and smiled.

"Hey, everyone," she said, waving at the screen when friends and family began popping onto the live. There were the usual friends from college as well as some new ones she'd made at the bachelorette party. "I made it to Germany! So far, this trip is pretty ah-may-zing."

It'd better be. She'd rolled the dice and went with what her heart wanted instead of the boring and practical accounting job she'd walked away from. Maybe this assignment would finally prove to her parents that she could make a living as a photographer so they'd stop the constant badgering about returning to the family business. Granted, boring and practical paid the bills, but photography filled her soul. A chance to make a living at it beyond selling prints here and there on social media was priceless, and life was too short to waste on working a job that sucked her soul dry.

She wove her way through the crowd as best she could. Thank God for her T-shirt dress and lace-up Vans. It was like wearing a nightshirt in public, only more stylish and socially acceptable.

"You guys, this airport is huge. When I get over to baggage claim, I'll show you." She quickly read one of the comments on her screen. "Oh, hey, Tina. For those of you who don't know, Tina's my bestie, and let me tell you, the girl can throw a bachelorette party, especially when it's her own." The comments section exploded with chatter, asking for details. She laughed. "I'm going to let her fill you in, but to answer her question, my first photo shoot is tomorrow. In Switzerland." The word rolled off her tongue all right, but it was still too freakin' incredible to believe. "I'll post sneak peeks, obviously."

The conversation turned toward the bachelorette party as she maneuvered her roller bag onto the escalator, careful not to tip it over. It'd likely take down the nun two steps down. And live on Instagram. Yeah, not a good marketing move.

Once in baggage claim, she headed for the closest wall and plastered herself out of the way. Her brother's flight should've gotten in an hour ago, and with any luck, both Jackson and her photography gear would be waiting somewhere easy for her to spot, even in this thick crowd.

"Here, you guys have to see this."

She tapped the screen to flip the camera around and panned the cavernous space packed with travelers, some looking harried as they rushed across the room while others strolled along like they were happy to be home.

Jackson was somewhere in this crowd with her camera pack. If she hadn't had to haul a bunch of stuff to Tina's bachelorette party, she'd have taken her precious camera herself. But Tina had also made it clear: Zandra was there to have fun. No photos allowed. It was like cutting off a limb, but she'd finally agreed.

Which was probably why she was so antsy to meet up with her brother. As part of Army Special Forces, he'd been all over Europe while she'd traveled no farther than Chicago. And that was just two days ago.

"My brother is in here somewhere." She scanned the crowd a moment longer then glanced at the screen. "Wait, what? I missed a hot guy? Where?" Leave it to her new friends from the bachelorette party to pick out a hot guy in the middle of a crowded airport. "Here, let me zoom in so we can all get a better...look..."

What the...?

"Oh crap."

Zandra blinked. The guy was the clichéd tall, dark, and handsome, all right. And he was headed straight for her, an amused smile on his lightly bearded face that mirrored the one he'd shot her way a couple of days ago in Seattle, just before she'd left for the airport. The comments came pouring in.

Oh crap? Wait do you recognize him or something?
OMG he's soooo hot. And he's coming your way!
Please tell us you know him.

And then from Tina, *Is that who I think it is?*

She swallowed. "Yep. That's Blake, my brother's best friend."

And given the way he strode toward her, all two hundred pounds of purpose, her camera pack slung over his broad shoulder, Zandra was pretty sure she wasn't going to like what was about to go down.

Chapter Two

There wasn't a thing Blake Monroe wouldn't do for Jackson. Unfortunately, his best bud recognized that fact, even though Blake planned to spend most of his four weeks of leave building a wall unit for his mother's apartment and making small repairs around the place. The fact that his mom had pretty much told him to go away because she had a chemistry exam to study for and a human physiology paper to write? Well, that only added salt to the wound.

Which meant Blake was free, as far as Jackson was concerned—never mind the concert tickets he'd given up to go on this trip—so Blake was now set to protect Jackson's little sister as she traipsed through Europe then safely deliver her back to Seattle in twelve days.

He shook his head. For all their wealth, her parents didn't travel anywhere that required stepping foot onto an airplane, which meant Zandra knew little about domestic travel, let alone traveling internationally. At least she'd been smart enough to recognize it and accepted her brother's help. And now Blake would be taking his place.

Consider it a mission, Jackson had said.

Blake took missions very seriously. Jackson knew that, too.

He glanced at the wide-eyed look Zandra cast his direction, along with the phone she held pointed at him, and blew out a breath. For once it'd be nice if she'd put the damn thing away and quit curating every move she made like it was a huge part of history. Why she felt her life had to be an open book was beyond him.

By the time he reached her, she'd ditched the phone, tucking it into the front pocket of her long T-shirt, if you could even call it that. The shirt hung down just low enough to cover half her thighs and exposed long, cream-colored legs, yet it was enough to make a guy wonder what was underneath it.

God knew Blake had been guilty of wondering since coming back to Seattle on leave. Sometime over the years, Zandra had grown from a scrawny girl in braces into one hell of a gorgeous woman. She'd filled out in all the right places and…

Whoa. What the hell was he doing? Zandra York was off-limits—for obvious reasons. Not the least of which being that she was his best friend's little sister.

"Blake," she said, pushing off from the wall and looking past his left shoulder. "Where's Jackson?"

"Well, hello to you, too, sunshine."

She pursed her mouth into a thin line. "Sorry. Sleep deprived, and I wasn't expecting you." She peered around him. "This is a joke, isn't it? Jackson's hiding somewhere getting a hell of a laugh, right?"

Yeah, figured she'd see it that way. But given the pranks they'd pulled on her over the years, Blake wasn't too surprised.

"He said he'd talk to you." Actually, Jackson had said he'd *try* to talk with Zandra before he left for the field. "I take it that didn't happen."

He shifted the camera bag onto his other shoulder. If he'd had his way, he'd have shoved her gear into his backpack, but Jackson had warned him how touchy Zandra got when it came to her photography equipment.

"Nope." She crossed her arms in front of her and stared at him. "I'm really too tired to play twenty questions. Just, please, tell me where Jackson is."

He cleared his throat. "Remember that special assignment he was waiting to hear about? The one that he'd gotten clearance from so he could go with you on this trip?"

She blinked those pretty blue eyes. "Yes. He promised me it was a done deal."

"His CO changed her mind." Wouldn't be the first time. The woman was badassed and took no prisoners when it came to advancing her career or the reputation of her team. Blake was just glad he trained Special Forces operatives and had a halfway decent Commanding Officer.

Zandra blew out a breath. "So, by now he's somewhere halfway across the world."

"Maybe. They don't exactly disclose secret stuff like that."

He rubbed his hands together and looked around. "So, world-famous photographer, you ready to grab your suitcase and head to Stuttgart?" He glanced at his watch. One thing he'd learned to bank on was the efficiency of the German train schedule. "The next train should be here in about an hour, just enough time to grab your stuff, clear customs, and get to the train station."

She shook her head. "Wait. That's it? Jackson's not here, but you are, so we just go on our merry way? He asked you to stand in, didn't he?"

"Yep. You got any other suggestions? This is your gig, after all." He shifted his weight from one foot to the other. "I wouldn't mind heading back to Seattle." Even if his mother was too busy, there were still things he could fix around her apartment—like the leaky faucet she didn't want to report for fear of her rent going up.

Zandra shook her head and pushed a lock of blonde hair out of her face, then she studied him a moment, those gorgeous eyes assessing. Damn, but he was tempted to return the favor. It was bad enough he'd noticed her legs at all.

"As. If," she muttered like she'd read his mind. "I've been handed an opportunity, and I'm not walking away from it."

Yeah, she'd sure changed from Jackson's pesky little sister into one amazingly sexy, talented, intelligent woman. And if he knew what was good for him, Blake would back the hell off.

He scrubbed a hand over his face. Maybe Zandra wasn't the only one suffering from jet lag. His brain was definitely harder to control once it hit the Zandra zone.

"Let's grab your suitcase."

He led the way through the crowd, skirting past a family with three kids in a stroller and the poor bastard who was strapped down with bags as well as the cart that held a mound of suitcases. If the guy looked this defeated just starting his vacation, Blake hated to see what he'd look like after.

One thing was for sure, Blake wouldn't fall into that trap anytime soon. He had huge life plans, ones that involved getting his mother through med school before he left the Army and settled down to start his own life trek.

Anything he went through until then was worth it, even spending the next week and a half babysitting Zandra. This was just another mission—nothing more. He needed to remember that every time his brain wanted to head down Zandra Lane and fantasize about all the ways she could wrap her legs around him.

Fuck. Blake gave himself a mental shake.

Special Forces training specialist my fucking ass. He had

better focus than what he'd shown so far.

He sucked in a deep breath. Okay, time to regroup.

All he had to do was keep her safe and haul her shit around. He just hoped he could eventually convince himself of that.

Chapter Three

Zandra peered into the mirror and applied another coat of mascara. Other travelers passed behind her, rushing off to the next leg of their journey. If her brother were here, she'd be just as anxious. The trip could even be considered fun, given that he was prone to finding adventure in just about anything—the kinds that they'd never experienced growing up, thanks to their overprotective parents.

Only now Jackson wasn't here and she was stuck with his best friend instead.

Wasn't that just special?

She stared at her reflection and took a deep breath. This was her first trip abroad, she didn't speak the language, and she wasn't familiar with taking a train. Not even the Seattle Center monorail. Anything beyond figuring out Google Maps would likely land her in Russia instead of Stuttgart. Hell, even Google Maps was a challenge.

All of these were reasons why she'd planned for her brother to come along. She'd get the hang of it all eventually—hopefully—but the last thing she needed was to be a frazzled, lost mess until she did.

Not that she wasn't up for some adventure, but right now she had to concentrate on why she was here: she needed to take this first real assignment and make it work. It was the only way to finally prove to the world—aka, her parents—that she could follow her dream and still feed herself.

One step at a time. It was like helping her former clients control costs so they could grow their businesses, only this time, she was applying these principles herself. She might not have a lot of financial resources, but she was happy, and that's what mattered most.

A group of uniformed, teenaged girls entered, banded together with chatter in a language Zandra didn't understand. Still, she smiled. It wasn't that long ago when she and her friends went everywhere together and did everything together, when they laughed and shared all kinds of secrets. And then they grew up and scattered, each leaving Seattle and following her own path. Everyone except Zandra—until now.

The group walked past, and someone bumped into her, jolting her forward a bit so the tip of her mascara wand smudged against a white band on her dress. "Oh, no."

One of the girls stopped and smiled apologetically. "Sorry."

She said something to another girl in the group, and soon Zandra took the paper towel offered her.

"That's okay." She dabbed at the front of her dress. "It'll come off."

With a smile and what Zandra assumed to be apologies, the girls left.

She shrugged. A black smudge on her dress wasn't that big a deal in the grand scheme of things.

A few minutes later, she peered at her reflection and grinned. There. That was so much better. She no longer looked like she'd just spent seven hours on a plane. Replacing her makeup bag in her crossbody bag, she glanced down at the gaping outer pocket of her camera bag. Wait. When did she… "Oh, shit."

• • •

Blake surreptitiously studied the crowd of people rushing past him like he was a rock off to the side of his favorite hiking trail.

Kind of like how he felt about his life.

He stuffed down the inevitable feeling that he wasn't moving fast enough and affected a bored look instead. Studying people was an occupational hazard, which was partly why the group of schoolgirls caught his eye. They looked innocent enough, but he knew that the most successful thieves were unassuming and often banded together, making them more efficient.

Following the group was a man with a little boy riding on his shoulders. The child had a huge grin and hung onto his dad's head with both hands as they made their way through the crowd. Blake stared, unable to tear his gaze away, and the memories of being with his own father floated from the past. The pang was sudden, intense, hitting him in the chest like an unexpected blow that almost took his breath away.

He sucked in a glob of air and stuffed the memory back. There was no room for it. Not now. Not ever. Not if he wanted to move forward and not wallow in the past.

Focus.

The command made Blake reach down for the pink-flowered suitcase Zandra had left with him. Yeah, it was still there.

Okay. The pain subsided, and he trained his gaze on the group of schoolgirls again. Suspicious-looking teens were outside the parameters of this mission.

Blake pulled his backpack off his shoulder and locked it between his feet. Waiting for Zandra was taking way longer than he'd expected, although he really shouldn't be surprised. She was a woman, after all. A beautiful, talented, albeit misguided woman. Who'd walk away from a successful family business that was practically being handed over to her?

Sure, Jackson had, too, but he was better at looking down a sniper's scope than tapping a keyboard. Blake couldn't imagine his best friend stuck in an office all day.

Maybe it was the same for Zandra.

He turned at the flash of white and hot pink in a sea of dark colors. Finally. At the wide-eyed look Zandra shot him, he pushed off from the wall and reached down for his backpack. "What's wrong?"

"My lens." She indicated the camera bag she'd insisted on hauling with her like another limb. "It's missing."

He frowned. "I brought you everything Jackson handed me. Maybe you forgot to pack it?"

She shook her head. "There were these girls, a whole group of them...I think...maybe..."

Her words trailed away as Blake turned in the direction he'd seen the group go. "Stay here. Watch your stuff."

"Hey! Where are you going?"

He ignored her as he wound his way through the crowd, past some damned family that was holding a meeting in the middle of the damned train station corridor.

He doubled down on his search. Those girls couldn't have gotten very far. Then again, they were thieves who likely knew the Frankfurt train station by heart.

Frustration split through him in spades, and he shoved a hand through his hair. There was a chance the group had blown into the station with no intention of catching a train at all and simply left. They could be anywhere by now.

Damn it. It was his first hour with Zandra and he'd already allowed something bad to happen. At this rate, he was going to fail his mission before it even began.

Chapter Four

By the time Blake returned, Zandra had half wondered if he'd abandoned her. Not that she believed he truly would. The guy was overprotective to a fault, only this time, there was something comforting in the knowledge that he was with her.

Blake swung the backpack off his shoulder, his movements jerky, his gaze dark and pinned on hers. "I thought I told you to keep your stuff close."

She bristled at the tone of his voice. "I did. I had it on the floor and stepped through the strap so no one would walk away with my bag, just like you told me. How was I supposed to know someone would try to steal anything with me standing over it like that?"

Intensity rolled off of him in spades. "Look, I'm sorry I didn't catch up with them, but now you know that I really mean it when I say you need to be aware of everything around you. *Everything.*"

"Because we're not in Kansas anymore?"

"I'm serious, Zandra."

She held up her hands in mock defeat. "Okay, okay, you've made your point. I'll watch my stuff more closely."

He frowned. "You know, for someone who's just had something stolen, you're pretty calm about it."

"For someone who *didn't* just have something stolen, you're pretty intense about it," she countered, unable to keep the irritation out of her voice. "It's bad enough the lens cost a lot of money, but what the hell am I supposed to do about it now? Yell? Scream? Tear my hair out?" She glared. "I don't have time for any of that."

She reached for the handle of her suitcase. "I'm chalking this up to a Life 101 lesson because there's nothing constructive to be done. Besides, that was an extra lens, a long-range one I'd packed in case an opportunity came up, but it isn't integral to the assignment." Thank God.

Most of what *Flights and Sights* wanted were staged photos. Not her favorite, but she'd give them what they wanted. They were, after all, paying her. She'd just take extras for herself.

Blake led her out of the stream of travelers and pulled a combination lock off his pack. "Here," he said, handing it over. "I should've slapped this on your photo bag before I even got on the plane."

"Would you stop with the guilt thing, already? It wasn't your fault, I can take care of myself, and I don't need your overprotective ass hovering over me this entire trip."

"Too bad." He held the lock out. "Jackson made it very clear that I was in charge."

She crossed her arms and stared. "Seriously? Not even *he* would have been in charge."

He blew out a breath then eased in another one. "Look. Let's just agree that, since this is your first time abroad, you need my help, okay? And I'll promise not to hover if you promise to take my instructions seriously."

Seemed reasonable. "Deal." She took the lock from him. "What's the combo?"

There was a flash of something indescribable in his toffee-brown eyes. "427," he said abruptly.

She stared at him and tilted her head to one side. "427," she repeated. The numbers felt familiar, but she couldn't place them. She snapped the lock on and stood. "What are you going to do without one?"

"I'll manage," he said smoothly, taking her suitcase. "Our train platform's this way, and the Germans are sticklers for staying on schedule, which means we've got less than ten minutes."

"I've got it," she said, reaching for the handle. "I hauled it over here, so it's not like I can't take care of it."

He hesitated, then shrugged. "Fine. Suit yourself. Just don't tell my mom that I didn't offer."

With her roller bag in one hand and her suitcase in the other, Zandra took a deep breath.

She had every intention of suiting herself, thank you very much. She'd make this travel assignment a monumental success because she had to.

At least, that was the plan.

• • •

It was completely stupid of Blake to not have changed the lock combination shortly after keying it in the first place. What kind of idiot was he, anyway? Army life was all about details. Details were what kept a soldier safe, and while he wasn't anywhere near the front lines these days, he knew details mattered. Like now. At least Zandra hadn't seemed to notice.

He cast a glance her direction, noted the way she sat with her face practically plastered to the train window, her phone out and recording the scene as it flew past, and caught the hint of a smile as she turned. "Look at that old church. How cool. I love old churches."

"How come?"

"I don't know. Something almost...mystical about them, I suppose."

She quickly posted the video to her Instagram and went back to gazing out the window at the passing countryside and the occasional small towns they'd passed along the way. It was a scene he was familiar with, given the amount of time he'd spent in Germany on his last tour. Of course, the majority of it was spent instructing the United Nations Special Forces out of Belgium, but he'd managed to hop a train to wherever, whenever he got the chance. Oftentimes he was alone, free to travel on his own schedule, and he preferred it that way.

She oohed and grabbed for her phone again as something caught her eye. Sunlight bounced off of the top of her head as she moved, and he fought a sudden need to reach out and touch her hair. Soft. It was probably as soft as it looked, silky, even, and would slide through his fingers...

He blinked. What the hell? Blake inhaled sharply and braced his hands on his thighs. This was Zandra, for Christ's sake.

Off-limits.

Hot-as-fuck.

Zandra.

He gripped his thighs to stop from reaching for her. If he were honest with himself, he'd admit that he liked her so damned much, it'd been eating at him for a while now.

And although he and Jackson had never discussed the possibility of Blake pursuing Zandra, he was pretty sure he'd be breaking a Bro Code somewhere in there.

Which left him, where? Back where he started. He was on a mission to escort her on her photojournalism assignment, to act as her assistant when needed, and also to make sure she got home safely. He needed to keep his head on straight and his dick in his pants.

Should be simple enough if he could remember all the reasons to keep her at arm's length. He ran them through his head again to re-center himself.

First, even if there wasn't some Bro Code that led to Jackson gutting Blake for looking twice at Zandra, Blake knew their lives were on a different trajectory. While she was just starting a new career that involved traveling the world, he was more than ready to leave the Army and settle down. In fact, the only reason he re-enlisted was because of his mother.

Second, he had a Life Plan, damn it, starting with getting his mother through med school. He owed her, and every spare nickel he had was earmarked to helping her achieve her dream.

The third? He needed to get his own ass through law school. There were people out there who needed to be prosecuted when they were caught, with justice brought to those unable to defend themselves. He'd always wanted that job. And one day, he'd have it.

Which meant that until he got himself through law school, he had nothing to offer a woman, especially someone like Zandra.

This was going to be a long trip.

"How much longer?"

Her question jarred him out of his thoughts—what, was she a mind reader now?—but it was the raised hands over her head and the slow stretch that short-circuited his brain.

She frowned and lowered her arms. "Until Stuttgart. How much longer?" she asked when he simply stared.

He blinked and pulled out his phone. "Another forty-five or so. You tired?"

"Yeah. I was pretty tired when I boarded the plane from

Chicago, and sleeping was pretty much non-existent." She yawned.

"How was the bachelorette party?" The more he talked, maybe the less he'd think. It was worth a shot, given the quality of his thoughts at the moment.

Zandra smiled, and damn if her face didn't glow. At least, she lit up in a way that teased Blake, made him wonder, made him want to see how often he could make her smile. "It was the best time."

She shook her head, and her grin widened. "I swear we didn't sleep more than a few hours the entire weekend. Like, total cat naps here and there, especially after the male strippers and the G-string incident the night before I left."

The sound of her light giggle tugged at something deep in his chest and made him want to see how often he'd be able to tease one out of her.

"I'm not sure I need to know about the G-string incident." He pulled his backpack toward him and propped an elbow on it. "Especially where naked dudes are involved."

She got that look in her eyes, the one that said he was about to be challenged. "You got something against naked dudes?"

"In case you hadn't noticed, I'm a dude, but I'm not into dudes, naked or otherwise."

There was that grin on her face again, the one that he was almost sure would get him into trouble one day.

"Fair enough." She shrugged. "I just thought you might want some insight into what women like. You know, since you most likely date women since you're not into dudes and all."

"I have a feeling you're going to tell me all about the debauchery that went on, so let's get it over with." He slumped against the seat, careful to keep his hand firmly on the backpack beside him. Maybe it was dumb giving up his padlock, but he was much better at keeping his stuff secured than Zandra would know to be. She was smart, though, and she'd pick it up quickly.

"It wasn't debauchery, it was a bachelorette party. And I'm happy to report the bachelorette was thrilled that her bridesmaids had as good a time as she did. I just wish Tina hadn't banned my camera. Although there really was good reason to not want evidence."

"Did no one think to use a phone?"

"Oh, she made sure we gave them up before we started. Smart lady." Then Zandra let out a small laugh. "Did you know elephants have relatively small penises?"

He cocked his head to one side. "Why do you feel the need to tell me this?"

"You know that old saying about how size doesn't matter?" she asked, clearly ignoring his question. "Well, it's apparently true in some parts of the world."

Her face cracked into a smile that soon broadened again. But her eyes were what captured Blake. They practically sparked with mischief, and he shifted uneasily in his seat. Damn. If he didn't know any better, he'd swear she planned to make this trip harder than it should be.

"Am I going to be subjected to penis talk until we get to Stuttgart? Because maybe I should hop off this train and head back to Seattle."

"Oh, stop whining," she said, settling back against her seat. "Seriously, though, Tina's going through with this whole marriage thing, and I'm not sure I get it. She's got a couple more years of law school, so why they don't wait doesn't make sense."

Well, she had him there. She was talking to someone chomping at the bit to get into law school, only she didn't know that. No one did. Not even his mother.

"Then again, love knows no time." She sighed, her shoulders raising then lowering.

"I never pegged you for a romantic."

She turned her head just far enough to eye him. "You make it sound like a bad thing. It's not, you know."

"No need to get defensive. I just thought that you were a numbers kind of girl."

"Yeah, well, those came in handy in the accounting world, but that doesn't mean I don't have a more idealistic view of life, and it doesn't mean it's a bad thing, either."

"Granted." He nodded his head slightly. "So, go on, tell me about this romantic bachelorette weekend."

"It wasn't the weekend that was romantic, it was the—oh, never mind. You wouldn't get it."

"No, seriously, try me."

"You sure?"

"We've got a while to Stuttgart, so consider me your captive audience."

She hesitated then nodded as if deciding he meant it. "Tina's jumping the gun a bit by marrying John when she's only got a couple more years, but life's too short to not do what you love, what pulls at your soul to be the best you can be, you know? Even if it does mean giving up your personal freedom." She cringed. "I guess..."

"What about responsibility? What about playing the long game so you see what's really best for you—and others? Life's not just about one person." Blake knew that better than anyone.

"True, it isn't. But how much can you fulfill someone else's dreams when you haven't fulfilled your own, and... Why are you grinning?"

"This." He pointed a finger, alternating between the two of them. "This is the kind of conversations I remember having with you when we were growing up. That's why I don't think of you as a romantic, a dreamer, an idealist, even."

She lifted her chin. "Yeah, well, I'm working on Zandra

version 2.0, and nothing's going to stop me from getting where I want to go in life."

"Zandra 2.0, huh? Is that, like, an upgrade?"

"More like a reboot. And this time, I'm going to do what I want." She stared at him. "What about you? Why are you here?"

"Like, now? On a train with you to Stuttgart? Or something more metaphysical like, why do I exist? Because if it's the latter, it might take me a while to come up with an answer."

She rolled her eyes. "Why did you come when Jackson couldn't?"

Good question, but hardly one he'd answer with, "Because your brother made me." It was far more complicated than that. "Like Jackson, I believe in you, in supporting your dreams as you reach for them with both hands." It was true. Even if Jackson hadn't volun-told him, there was a fairly good chance Blake would've stepped up anyway.

Of course, that was before he realized just how strong the pull toward Zandra would be.

"Tina's calling the shots for her life, not conforming to what's expected, but living life on her terms. She did it when she moved to Chicago and again when she decided to marry John now instead of waiting the way her parents wanted her to."

Blake didn't know about any of that stuff, but he did know one thing: Tina's move to Chicago gave her and John the best chance to make their relationship work. He knew from watching his Army buddies that military life was hard, even if a spouse moved to where a soldier was posted. But to try and carry on a long-distance relationship? Well, he didn't have any stats on that, but he was willing to believe that a relationship was more likely to fail than thrive.

She stared out the window. "Tina's the one who inspired

all this," she said softly. "The one who made me realize that there would never be the 'perfect' time to chase my dreams, especially where my parents are concerned."

Blake sat up straighter then shifted in his seat. He had his own opinions about the York parents, but now probably wasn't the time to bring them up. "That why you quit?"

She faced him, an eyebrow raised. "Thank you for acknowledging that, and yes, that's why I quit their accounting company." Zandra slumped against the seat. "Honestly, sometimes I feel so ungrateful, you know? Like my parents had done so much for me, had given me such a head start, and here I am thumbing my nose at it, at them."

Whoa. He might've agreed with her, but what would be the point? Besides, this was getting way too deep. He cleared his throat. "The important thing is that you're doing what you want, not what's expected of you."

"Are you?" She focused her baby blue eyes on him and waited expectantly.

"Am I what?"

"Doing what you want? Is the Army all that there is for you?"

"No."

"Care to expand that thought?"

"No." This time *he* yawned and folded his arms across his chest, his backpack securely tucked between him and the side of the train. "I'm taking a nap. Wake me when we get to Stuttgart."

The last thing he wanted to do was get too close, too intimate, to anyone. Even a gorgeous blonde who had the guts to go after her dream, consequences be damned. One day, it'd be his turn. Blake just had to bide his time.

Chapter Five

Zandra blinked as the hotel clerk's words sank in, because of course she'd forgotten her brother had made the reservations after telling her not to worry about it. But since Jackson wasn't here, she was now sharing an extended stay room with Blake?

"That's not possible," she said for about the eighth time. "We can't stay in the same room together."

While she wouldn't have minded her brother sleeping on the sofa, she *definitely* minded that Blake would be there instead.

The older man glanced between the two of them. "We do have another room still available." He tapped on his computer keyboard then told them the cost.

Zandra rubbed her eyes and shook her head to clear it. Her funds were limited since the e-zine didn't give her much of an advance and had a cap on how much she'd be reimbursed. "I can't afford that," she said, blowing out a breath. It sucked to admit it, but it was the truth.

Great. Just. Great. She could almost see her mom's I-told-you-so face staring at her, followed by her father's what-were-you-thinking one. So far, this European adventure wasn't turning out quite the way Zandra had expected.

Blake chuckled beside her. "You're just afraid you can't keep your hands off me," he said, pulling out his wallet.

She slowly turned her head to face him. "The hell I can't." She could, couldn't she? She could share a room with Blake and keep her hands—and her body—to herself.

He grinned. "You still sleep in those princess shorts?"

"Oh my God. You remember that?" She felt her face heat. "It's been at least ten years."

"Maybe so, but something like that's hard to forget." He winked.

It'd been the middle of the night. Blake and her brother were home on winter break. She'd made a bathroom run at the same time Blake had, and by the time she'd stopped gaping at his bare chest, she realized he'd done his fair share of looking at her, too.

"My mom bought those for me. If it weren't for the fact that I hadn't gotten around to doing my laundry, I wouldn't have—" Zandra propped her hands on her hips and blew out a breath. Oh, brother. Why was she even trying to explain herself? That was more than ten years ago.

"For what it's worth, your legs are still perfect."

His quietly whispered words drifted toward her, and she quickly glanced up and caught his powerful gaze. It was as if he reached across the short distance between them and lightly caressed her, a cascade of tingles tumbling through her system.

Then, as if he'd realized what he'd said, Blake stepped back, opened up his wallet, and cleared his throat. He slapped a credit card on the counter. "I'll get my own room."

Zandra reached out and grabbed the card before the hotel clerk could take it. "Not so fast. What makes you think you're

God's gift to a sane woman? I wouldn't know what your track record is with women—and not that I care, honestly—but I know that I most definitely am not tempted to"—she looked around them, noted the relatively empty foyer, and leaned forward—"go *there*." She straightened and held his gaze. "You can sleep on the couch."

"What if I want the bed?" he countered. "You willing to give that up?"

Zandra was tempted to call in the "be a gentleman" card, but she'd fought so hard for an equal chance to prove she could do the kinds of things her brother had been allowed to do. Blake knew it, and there was no way she was walking back her claim to save herself from some discomfort.

Damn him.

But that didn't mean she couldn't lay down terms of her own. "Tell you what." She leaned a hip against the reception desk and ignored the clerk who undoubtedly was watching their exchange with morbid curiosity. "I'll give you an opportunity to switch places. How's that?"

"An 'opportunity,' huh? What exactly does that mean?"

"It means just that—do a little something extra as my assistant, and we'll call the switch a bonus for a job well done."

The corner of his mouth twitched up slightly. She searched her brain for some sort of a solution, something that wouldn't make her look prissy or weak because no way in hell was she either of those things.

"Okay." Blake took his credit card from between her fingers. "You're on."

"Deal."

Even as she said the word, Zandra had a sneaking suspicion it would be harder than she'd thought.

• • •

Blake switched on the room light and stepped aside to let Zandra pass, her floral scent trailing behind her.

God, she fucking smelled good, too. He must be some special kind of dumb to not have insisted on his own room.

Of course, bringing up the night he'd seen her with a skimpy pair of shorts and see-through top wasn't a good idea. But did his brain hear that? Hell no. It went with what his dick was thinking instead.

Stupid dick.

She set her crossbody bag on the bed. "This will work."

He let the door close and followed her in.

Remember the mission.

The mission. Right. He had to get her to her photo shoots, he had to keep her safe, and he had to get her home. That was his job. And after the way someone was able to easily take her camera lens from her, it was probably a really good idea not to let Zandra out of his sight.

The woman in question had pulled out her phone again and was taking a quick video of the room. Did people actually find this stuff interesting?

He dropped his backpack by the couch and glanced at the small kitchen. "Want some food? I can grab something from the corner store."

"Ummm…sure. I guess."

She licked her lips as she typed out something on her phone, and his gaze was drawn to the slow sweep of her tongue, to the way it gently glided over full, red lips. Damn, he needed air. Fast.

He was at the door in two strides. "Why don't you go ahead and get settled in? I'll get us something for tonight and breakfast tomorrow." Because even the sorry excuse of a kitchen was reason enough to keep his hands and his brain busy.

Chapter Six

Zandra stared at the closing door and took a deep breath. What just happened? Not only did Blake morph into the hottest guy she'd ever seen, but they still got each other the way they used to. Like back before he went off to college and totally ignored her. Which was fine at the time, but now...

Her brain kicked into gear. Busy. Zandra needed to stay busy or she ran the risk of jumping Blake, which wouldn't be the best way to start her assignment. You know, the one her whole future depended on?

Which was why she'd tossed her phone onto the bed without even reading her notifications, quickly unpacked her bags, then made a beeline for the shower.

By the time she'd pulled the bathroom door open in a swirl of steam, she knew Blake was back. The delicious smells coming from the kitchen were a dead giveaway, and her stomach grumbled. When was the last time she'd eaten anything that wasn't pre-packaged with an airline logo on it? The margaritas she'd had at the bachelorette party the night before she left didn't count, either. Unfortunately.

She glanced down at her nightshirt. For bumming around the hotel room with her brother, it was no big deal. With her brother's best friend, well… She let out a breath. On Jackson's advice, she'd kept her wardrobe to a minimum, which meant there wasn't even a pair of shorts she could wear with it, and she sure wasn't putting on a pair of jeans, either.

Screw it. The nightshirt was almost as long as the T-shirt dress she'd worn on the trip over. She'd live.

She towel-dried her hair as she walked toward the kitchen, considered styling it, and immediately squashed the thought. What was she thinking? This was Blake. Bothersome, overprotective, pain-in-the-butt Blake. The same guy who was here out of obligation, nothing more.

Still, her mouth watered when she rounded the corner, and it wasn't just what he was cooking, but it was Blake himself. He stood by the stove, one hand whisking up something in a bowl, while the other hand slowly poured a stream of oil into it.

Strange how the frilly apron didn't detract from the pure maleness of the man who wore it. His magnetism seemed to reach out to her, taunting her into wondering if she'd survive the night with him on the couch just a few feet away.

He turned. "Hey. Do you still drink hot chocolate?"

"Only if there are marshmallows in it."

"Some things never change." He grinned and reached for a mug. "Fortunately for you, I remembered and picked some up. Give me a sec to heat up some milk."

Aw, that was cute. He'd remembered she liked marshmallows. She stepped into the room as he set a small pot on the stove. "Where did you learn to cook?"

That was good. Cooking was a neutral subject. A good subject. Evocative of substances that nourished the body in the same way that a kiss had the power to nourish the soul.

Good God, that's cheesy. Zandra rolled her eyes at her

own observation and continued to towel her hair.

"Learned as soon as I could hold a knife," he said, opening the oven door and reaching for something in it. "It was a way I could help my mom when she worked late. This looks like it's done. Hope you like eggs."

Zandra blinked at the skillet he set on the stovetop. "A frittata is a bit more complicated than just eggs."

He shrugged. "They're still just eggs to me. I learned different ways to prepare them since we always had eggs in the house."

"No kidding." She stepped closer. "This looks amazing. Are those spinach leaves? And mushrooms? And *cheese*?"

He wiped his hand on a towel and threw her a quick glance. "Not just any cheese, blue cheese."

Zandra's stomach grumbled in approval. "My favorite." She searched the counter behind him.

"I know. There's extra in the fridge."

She blinked. He remembered she liked blue cheese, too? And not only had he remembered, he'd put it in the dinner he'd made and even had a little extra for her to nibble on later. A tide of warmth started in her chest and emanated out. Was he always this sweet and she hadn't noticed?

For the love of all things holy, it was just marshmallows and cheese.

Chastising herself, she headed back to the bathroom to hang up her towel then stared at her reflection. "Remember why you're here. The assignment, your future, depends on this trip."

Right.

Besides, Blake wasn't the kind of guy she wanted in her life. Just like their names, they were on opposite ends of the spectrum. He couldn't understand her creativity, and she'd lived the straight-arrow boring life already. It wasn't for her ever again.

She finally had the freedom to do life on her terms, and she had a lot of time to make up. "That does not include a guy." Even one as yummy and unexpectedly thoughtful as Blake.

She blinked as her cell phone rang beside her, and practically jumped on the thing like she was afraid it'd get away.

"Jackson. Finally," she said, plugging in her earbuds.

"Hey. Guess you know I'm not there."

"Thanks for stating the obvious. You could've told me before, given me some sort of warning."

"Like you'd have agreed to it." He snorted.

Well, what was she supposed to say to that? Thanks?

"Listen, Squirt, I support you as best I can. You know that."

"I know." She leaned a hip against the bathroom counter.

"You're talented. You've got what it takes to make it as a photojournalist."

"Wish Mom and Dad could see that." Even now, pain mixed with a sense of defiance, which was silly. This was her life, not theirs.

"They just worry about you, that's all."

"So they don't worry about you?"

He chuckled. "You know better than that."

But they'd been supportive of Jackson, didn't insist that he join the family business the way they'd pressured Zandra. Thank goodness she'd gathered enough courage to go on her own anyway, even if it did take a couple years longer than she'd have liked.

"No doubt you've had it harder, Squirt, and I get that you want to do things on your own. But you've never traveled to Europe. That's why Blake's there."

"He's a pain in the ass."

"Just treat him the way you'd treat me."

"Like a pain in the ass big brother?"

"Exactly."

Her brain immediately transported her back to earlier, to their time in front of the reception desk, to the smoldering look and the zap of electricity that snared her.

Treat Blake like a brother? She cast a glance his direction. Even with his back to her, the guy was *hot*, frilly apron and all.

No way could she remotely think of him as a brother.

But she somehow had to.

She straightened and reached for a bottle of body lotion. The e-zine would get stellar photos from her, photos that would have them paying a huge bonus and begging to promote her to staff member instead of just a freelancer. There'd be even better assignments, bigger assignments, ones that would take her all over the world.

Come to think of it, *Flights and Sights* wasn't the only e-zine around, even though they were by far the largest. Still, she might be able to further her career by branching out and working for other publications. And if things worked out right, maybe, just maybe, Zandra would prove to her parents sooner, rather than later, that she was more than capable of making a viable living as a photographer.

After all, she could run her own life, thank you very much.

There was something really weird about making dinner for Zandra. Weird, but…right. Like, somehow, in this space and time Blake was doing exactly what he was meant to do.

He turned the oven off and shoved the rolls in to warm up. Topped with some sweet butter, they'd be perfect with the frittata. At least, he kinda hoped Zandra would see it that way. Did she eat things with butter these days? Some of the women he knew would rather eat cardboard than real food. Was Zandra one of them?

That was the other weird thing. Since when did he care what Zandra thought?

Ever since you ran into her in the middle of the night in those painfully short princess bottoms and practically non-existent tank top.

Four years separated them, and by the time he'd left for college, she'd been sixteen, little more than jailbait. Add to that that she was his best friend's little sister...well, it was a no-brainer *that* night.

So now here he was: twelve years later and still wondering what her body looked like underneath the skimpy clothing she chose to wear tonight.

He frowned. Didn't she bring any sweats? The way she moved in the oversize T-shirt was as damned sexy as the short shirt-dress thing she'd had on earlier. Trouble was, in this moment, watching Zandra move around the cramped room as she talked with her brother? Well...it was evocative of cozy evenings at home, maybe even watching TV after dinner. The kind of stuff he'd like to have in his life one day down the road.

And that wasn't the kind of life Zandra had planned. Where he wanted to settle down one day, she wanted to take photographs—all over the world. Which basically meant she wanted to live out of a suitcase. He was so done with living out of a duffel bag *now.* And he still had a couple more years to go.

Blake pulled two plates out of a cupboard and brought them to the small table with the lone bulb hanging over it.

He had to pull himself together and nix any thoughts of cozy evenings with Zandra. He glanced at her as she chatted on the phone and smothered lotion on her long legs.

Damn it.

Blake turned around and headed back to the frittata. Some way, somehow, he had to figure out how to keep his emotions in check and his brain in gear. For Zandra's good as well as his own.

Chapter Seven

"Is it possible to be jet-lagged and excited at the same time?"

Camera in hand, Zandra stared outside the train window at the passing scenery of green fields and clusters of trees that dotted the Swiss countryside. And to think they were in Stuttgart just a couple of hours ago. Clearly her brother's suggestion to base out of the German city had been a good one.

It was yet another example of how different their lives were. They might've started out with the same kind of childhood, but he'd clearly broken free and explored the world far more than she had. And so had Blake.

She adjusted the shutter speed and aperture then looked through the viewfinder, the train's movement naturally panning the shot as she snapped a photo of a farmhouse in the distance.

She was in Switzerland. Joy bubbled up inside her so hard and fast, she barely contained it. She was in Switzerland *on her first real assignment*. Freakin' *Switzerland*.

"Isn't this amazing?"

"I suppose," Blake said from beside her.

She set the camera on her lap. "I can't believe I'm here."

"Neither can I," he muttered.

She frowned at him. "What's the matter? Didn't you sleep well last night?" Come to think of it, he'd been pretty quiet since they'd gotten on the train.

"I'm fine." He crossed his arms, slid her a sideways glance, then looked away.

O-kay, then. Whatever he was dealing with was his problem, not hers. She stared out the window again. "Pinch me."

"You sure you want me to do that? I will, you know."

She turned, but there was no way she could muster up a frown. "This is just so freakin' cool!"

"Glad to see you're happy." Blake stretched his arms overhead, the movement emphasizing the way his T-shirt molded onto what were obviously perfectly formed pecs.

She tore her gaze from him and thumbed the window. "Let me guess. Gorgeous countrysides bore you."

He shrugged. "If you've seen one, you've seen everything there is."

She frowned. "You mean you're more concerned with protecting your backpack than looking at all this beauty? You're kidding, right?"

"No."

She huffed out a breath. This. This was the perfect example of why they couldn't be together, even a little. Not only was he mercurial with his moods, she couldn't see herself with a guy who could be bored with all the world had to share. No way. Not happening.

He pulled his ball cap over his eyes then hugged his backpack to his chest as if mocking her. "I'm taking a nap."

"Great." She pulled out her phone. "I'll put up another post."

He pushed the cap back up. "Instagram again?"

"You make it sound like I've spent the whole trip on social media."

"You kinda have."

"*Au contraire*, wise ass. I've only done one live at the airport yesterday, before you showed up, and a handful of stories." No posts. Which meant she was due for one sooner rather than later.

"Now, now, watch your language. That's not the kind of talk fitting for an up-and-coming world famous photographer."

"I don't know why you're so opposed to social media."

"I just don't think you need to advertise who you are. Let your work speak for itself."

"Oh, you terribly misinformed individual. That's not how the world operates these days. Success means engaging your followers so they'll continue to support your work. And if you're lucky, a huge e-zine like *Flights and Sights* will re-post your stories so you end up with even more followers." Zandra shifted. "Aren't *you* on Instagram?"

He shook his head. "No reason to be."

"Facebook?"

"No."

"Twitter?"

"Sorry to disappoint you, but no." He straightened and rearranged his Seahawks ball cap. "Look, I'm a soldier. I train Special Forces. Believe me, I don't need to advertise that."

That made sense. "Yeah, well, at least you get to pursue your dream."

"Working on it."

"Working on it?" Zandra frowned. That was a weird response. "Didn't you always want to be in the Army? At least, that's what Jackson said when he'd made the decision to enlist with you."

"Working on it," he repeated.

Clearly that topic was off-limits. Maybe time for another tactic. After all, if they were spending a lot of time together, didn't it make sense that she got to know him better?

"Did your mom raise you all by herself? I don't remember you talking about your dad. Or any other male figure for that matter."

"Twenty questions? Really?" He raised an eyebrow and glanced at the phone in her hand. "I thought you were doing a post."

She tucked the phone into a pocket of her backpack. "I just think it's really weird that I don't know all that much about you," she said, settling into her seat.

"Why would you?"

The question hung between them, and along with it an un-nameable...something. She swallowed and thought back to those years when Blake and Jackson first became friends. Sure, all three of them had laughed a lot and played pranks on each other. While she'd noticed him, he hadn't registered as anyone other than her brother's sidekick.

"We're four years apart, Zandra. By the time I'd left for college, you were starting your sophomore year and more into watching guys like Sean Devereaux play football."

Oh, yes, Sean Devereaux. Her teenaged hormones had zoned in on the 6'1" guy as soon as she'd seen him in a football jersey. "You remember that?"

"*Pfft*. He helped us win games. How could I forget?"

There was something he wasn't saying, something important, something that she couldn't quite put her finger on but was there nonetheless. "Yeah, well, I hear he's practicing law at his father's firm now."

"Good for him."

Zandra shrugged. "I suppose it's only natural to follow

in a parent's footsteps." Not that she thought it was natural. Why should she have her future chosen for her just because she was born into it?

"You'd be surprised."

Something in his tone caught her attention. "Was your dad in the military, too?"

"Yeah, he was a soldier but got out of the Army about the time my sister Lily was born." Blake blew out a breath. "Then he was killed a few months later defending a gas station attendant who was attacked by a bunch of thugs." His voice was low and eerie enough to make Zandra shiver. "They never did prosecute the bastards." He said it slowly, with a straight face and a matter-of-fact tone.

"That makes you around four when it happened." She'd gone to school with Lily, but they were little more than acquaintances. Where Zandra was into fashion and boys, Lily was reserved, spending most her time reading.

"Something like that." He stretched out his legs and nodded. "Fortunately, I had my grandfather around. That's why we moved back to Seattle, so he could help out while my mom went to work."

Zandra stared, tried to assimilate his words. Her own father drove her nuts, sure, but growing up without one? She couldn't imagine it, didn't want to imagine it. There was nothing she could say that didn't sound like a platitude, so she opted for sincerity. "Sounds like it was a rough time."

"It wasn't ideal." He shrugged. "But I wouldn't be who I am today without having had that experience."

She tilted her head to one side. "Wow. That's kind of deep."

He shrugged again but didn't offer anything more.

Zandra stared at Blake's profile, at the tilt of his chin and the way he turned and looked at her like she was the only other person in the train car. Just who was he, anyway?

The train slowed, signaling its entry into the next station, and Blake sat up. "Time to get off and switch trains." He grabbed his backpack. "Let's go."

What would it take to get him to drop his guard for just a few hours? To loosen up just long enough to know what really, truly made Blake Monroe tick?

She had a feeling he'd fight tooth and nail to keep that from her.

Chapter Eight

Blake climbed a set of stairs at the crowded train station, his gaze focused on the back of a petite older woman's gray head. He had no idea why he'd told Zandra that stuff about his dad, but the words were out before he could yank them back in. And now he felt vulnerable as hell.

He didn't like feeling vulnerable. In his line of work, vulnerability got you killed.

Not that this was a life or death situation, but still. Zandra made him *want* to be vulnerable. That was extremely inconvenient with him already struggling to keep her at arm's length.

Ahead of him, the older woman stumbled, her arms falling forward. Blake sprung into action, reaching out and grabbing onto both the older woman's shoulders, gently bringing her back to a standing position. "Are you okay?" he asked her once she was steady. "*Ganz langsam. Geht es Ihnen gut?*" His German wasn't that great, but he'd remembered a few phrases.

"*Danke zu sagen.* Thank you. I am fine," the older woman

supplied in perfect English. Given the part of the world they were in, he wasn't surprised. He'd often seen shop workers flow from one European language to another as easily as the customers who shopped.

The older woman touched her head and smoothed out a section of hair that had unraveled from its bun. "You are very kind."

"I am happy to help."

The woman began her ascent up the last few steps, and Blake followed at a close but not invasive distance. Just in case.

It wasn't until he reached the landing that he turned toward where Zandra was, just a few feet behind him on the top step. A corner of her full mouth tipped up in a smile as she stood there, the travelers climbing the stairs spilling around her, though she didn't seem to notice.

He couldn't help it. He adjusted his backpack and reached a hand out in silent invitation, the need to touch her, to hold her, to show her...something, anything meaningful overwhelming him to the point where he sucked in a deep breath. Damn, but it seemed hard to stay in control around her.

She extended her hand and grasped his, a reassuring smile on her face.

"You ready?" he asked with a slight squeeze of her hand.

Zandra simply nodded.

They said nothing more as they navigated the crowd, alone yet not alone in the sea of fellow travelers. Comfortable enough in the silence, their hands clasped together the only indication—a reassuring one—that they were in this thing together.

By the time they'd boarded the train and were settled in their seats, he'd deliberately let her hand go and forced his brain back to task. He didn't want his moment of weakness, of needing to touch her, to give her the wrong impression.

"So, you were telling me about your grandfather," she prompted as she reached for her camera bag.

You know, what he really ought to do was tell her it wasn't any of her business or else keep his answers brief. But that need to spill his guts to her, specifically, was still running strong.

So why the hell not? Really, it was no different than being with a battle buddy, was it? Someone you trusted to have your back in the thick of things, someone who, in those dark moments, you trusted enough to share your secrets with...in case you didn't make it back from a mission.

And while shooting photos in Europe was hardly close to a battle situation, the same principles applied. At least, that's what Blake told himself.

"My grandfather helped raise me," he finally said. Even after all this time, he felt his throat close, and he swallowed the dull ache away. "Mom was always trying to get me to sit still, but Gramps was the one who insisted I behave like a boy, doing all the normal stuff boys do."

She scrunched her nose. "There's no such thing."

"Yeah, well, that was a different time. Fishing, hunting, boating. We did it all." And every one of those excursions was a learning lesson so that Blake understood the value of self-control, of self-reliance, of self-belief. These became the building blocks of his Army life. Scratch that, of Blake's *whole* life.

"What about your dad?" she gently asked. "Do you remember much about him?"

He thought long and hard, and tried to conjure up the memory of the only man he'd called "dad." He didn't remember much other than there was a lot of laughter when his dad was still alive. His mom hadn't laughed much afterwards, and it'd only been in recent years—since she started college classes—that Blake had heard her deep-down laughter again. "Guess that's what happens when you reach for your dreams," he mumbled.

"Excuse me?" Zandra's quietly asked question broke through his thoughts, broke through the memories of those early days without his dad around.

"Nothing." He pulled the ball cap off and shoved a hand through his hair. "I was just remembering something, that's all."

She studied him closely, like she was trying to figure him out. "Oh. Well, like you said earlier, you're working to pursue your dream."

"Some of us have that opportunity." He shrugged again. "Others have to be patient, have to wait for something to open up for them, you know?" He sure as hell knew all about that one in spades.

"Sounds like you've got that part figured out."

"Do any of us, really? We go through life doing the best we can with what we've got. At the end of the day, that's all we can really do."

"That's for sure. Tell me something…" She drummed her fingers on the wood table between them and leaned forward. "Back there, with the little old lady, you do that kind of thing a lot?"

"Thing?"

"Help people out. Protect them. That kind of thing. You do that naturally, don't you?"

Interesting. He'd never really thought about it. "I guess."

A smile tugged at the corner of her lips. "So you're like the defender of the meek?"

Ha. He thought back to his last mission, the one before he'd been pulled to become a training specialist. Much as he hated to admit it, sometimes justice was best served at the end of a weapon, but he couldn't—and wouldn't—do that outside his role in the military. He would work within the constraints of the law.

"I'm more like a helper of those who need it." Especially those the justice system had failed—like his mom.

Which was why he'd chosen to pursue a career as a prosecuting attorney once he got the chance. At the rate his mother was going, he'd begin before he knew it.

He. Could. Not. Wait.

Chapter Nine

Zandra stared out the window and past the railroad tracks to the train station beyond. They were one train stop away from Lucerne now, and it shouldn't be too long before they were on their way again.

She yawned and stretched her arms above her head. Maybe she should take a quick nap, get herself well rested before she started the shoot. But there was something niggling in the back of her brain, something that was running in the background as she'd negotiated the last twenty-four hours. Not that she could do anything about it. If there was any chance of pulling it out while *wanting* to pull it out, whatever it was would have to flow free on its own.

"You're playing with your phone again," Blake said. "Are you going to do another of those live things?"

He sat across from her, an uber-sexy, lazy grin on his face as he cocked his head to one side. The guy was hands-down hot, all right. How she'd not noticed that before was a ridiculous oversight on her part.

"No. Actually, I'm going to do a post and a story." She

searched her phone's gallery and picked out a few choice photos from the selection of countryside, small towns, churches, and homes that lined the railroad tracks from Stuttgart. "There," she said as she uploaded them to her feed.

She held the phone out and hit the video icon. "We're on our way to Lucerne, but there's been a slight change of plans." She turned and panned the shot toward her companion. "This guy is now my travel buddy. Remember him from yesterday?" She switched the screen back and made a face. "Wish me luck." Chuckling, she ended the video.

She looked up and caught the slight frown on Blake's forehead. "What?"

"Did you just put me on your Instagram page?"

"Yeah. It's just a story, though," she said. "They're gone in twenty-four hours."

She pulled her backpack toward her...and there was that niggling feeling again. Her fingers touched the padlock Blake had insisted she put on her backpack yesterday. Without thinking, she turned each dial, stopping at each number with the kind of precision that would make her own parents proud—as if any of that counted at all.

As the numbers clicked into place in her brain, she raised her head until her gaze met Blake's. "The combination," she said, indicating the padlock in her hand. "This was the date I sold my first photograph."

His eyes widened slightly, then he shrugged. "Took you long enough to figure it out."

Wow. She wasn't wrong. That day had been amazing, in some ways just as good as the day a few weeks ago when she'd gotten word that *Flights and Sights* wanted to offer her a field position. "Why?" she finally asked. "Why would you choose that number?"

"Why not? I had to give you a number you'd remember."

His tone was cool, neutral, like maybe that really truly

was the reason. Except…

Zandra sat up in her seat and tilted her head to one side. "That'd make sense, only the combination was already set when you handed the padlock over yesterday."

"Maybe I set it on the plane, okay?"

"Okay, but—"

"Are we really going to talk about a particular combination?" He turned away, stared out the window to the train station beyond it, but not before she caught a flash of something in his eyes.

"Sure. Unless it's such a big deal that you'd rather not discuss it." She stared at him intently, not wanting to miss anything that would give some insight into his true feelings.

"I just remembered how excited you were about selling your first photo, that's all."

"Really? You didn't seem all that thrilled at the time."

"I was happy for you."

She'd hung out that night at Anthony's, one of her favorite spots near Pike Place Market, celebrating with her friends when Blake and her brother joined them. Actually, it looked more like Jackson had dragged Blake with him. "You looked like that was the last place you wanted to be that night."

"Maybe I'm just a good actor." He flashed her a cheesy grin.

"Nothing's outside the realm of possibility."

Zandra stopped as something blared over the train's speakers at the same time that Blake sat up, his face a mask as he listened.

"Damn," he muttered.

Other passengers in the compartment stood and gathered their belongings. "What's happening?" Zandra asked, a well of fear beginning in the pit of her stomach. "Why are they all getting up? Where are they going?"

Blake scrubbed a hand over his face. "We need to

disembark."

"What? Why? I have two hours to get to Lucerne then find Madame Pruissard's chocolate shop. We can't disembark now."

"Your choice." He stood. "You can sit here or we can find another way to get to Lucerne. Because right now, the train's not going anywhere since there's a problem with the railroad track about a couple miles ahead. We can't get through."

"Wait. What? That's not possible," she protested, her brain still struggling to comprehend how this could happen *now*, of all the damned times. "My photo shoot...they're waiting for me..."

She fought back the tide of panic, of the notion that she'd failed before she'd even started. What would she say to her parents? Jackson? *Flights and Sights*?

"Hey." Blake smiled, hefted his pack onto his back, and secured the straps around his waist. "We'll figure it out."

She took a deep breath, nodded, and replaced the lock on her backpack. "You're right. We'll figure it out."

In fact, she knew exactly what her next move would be.

• • •

Blake retraced his steps toward the front of the train station where he'd left Zandra. So much for getting any info out of train station officials. No one seemed to have a clue when the trains would be running again, and while he knew it wasn't necessarily the truth, he couldn't worry too much about that now.

He was like a salmon swimming upstream, against the stranded travelers that seemed to fill the entire building. But at the moment, there was only one stranded traveler he was concerned about.

He'd expected her to freak once she realized that they

couldn't continue. With any luck, the tracks would be replaced quickly, but who knew when it would happen? And while she'd raised her voice an octave or two, it wasn't half as bad as he'd thought it'd be. In the end, she was unexpectedly calm about it.

A corner of his mouth crooked up as he rounded the corner. He had to admit, he admired that about her.

Blake stopped, frowning at the now-empty area in front of him. No Zandra. This was where he'd left her—with explicit instructions not to move. He was sure of it. He scanned his surroundings. Yep, there was the train station's clock, and to the left were the reader boards that displayed arrival and departure times. This was exactly the place, only now she wasn't there.

He blew out his breath and grounded himself. It was the best way to think clearly, to come up with viable answers as to where she might have gone. She wasn't naïve—she wouldn't go off with anyone. Then again, she didn't stay put like she'd promised she would, either.

He raked his fingers through his hair and felt a trickle of sweat down the center of his back. Less than twenty-four hours and he'd lost a camera lens *and* Jackson's sister.

Maybe she'd gone to the restroom.

But three minutes—and a polite question to a woman leaving the restroom area—later, he ruled out a potty break.

Damn it.

He scanned the area again, forcing himself to concentrate on seeing Zandra's lucky white shirt, the one she'd insisted on wearing and had even taken the time to iron. Who the hell ironed a T-shirt?

No ironed T-shirt in sight.

Okay, he'd just call her. Problem solved.

He stopped, pulled out his cell phone, and groaned. No cell service. Fucking unbelievable.

Blake's irritation rose with each tick of the clock, with each face he studied as he searched through the crowd. When he found her—because he would—it'd take everything in him not to yell at her. Did she honestly think he wouldn't worry when she vanished into thin air? How hard was it to stay put for ten damn minutes?

Frustrated, he shoved his phone back into his pocket. Why the hell was he worrying in the first place? She was a grown woman. She didn't need a keeper.

Never mind that "Zandra's keeper" was essentially the definition of this mission.

Blake scanned the crowd again. There was a woman with a baby carriage. A man talking on his cell phone—lucky bastard. Two kids fighting while their parents stood close by, clearly ignoring them while they poured over a map.

Still no Zandra.

Blake stifled the irritation that raced through him and made himself breathe deeply. He could command a company of Special Forces soldiers with no problem. But Zandra? *Jesus.*

Chapter Ten

Zandra stood at the train platform, empty now save for the single row of parked trains extending back as far as she could see in one direction. Apparently even small towns got their fair share of train traffic.

She frowned. This totally sucked, but then again, the situation made for a great behind-the-scenes story. She framed the row of trains on her phone screen and snapped a photo, labeled it STRANDED, added a freaked-out sticker, and uploaded it.

She panned the rows of empty platforms and captured the distant sounds of train brakes. Another train stranded until the tracks were repaired. It wouldn't be long before a fresh batch of passengers disembarked. She stuck a nervous sticker on her video, tagged her location in Lucerne, and sent that off, too.

There. That was a start.

Quickly she turned the camera on herself. "Well, this is a set-back, but don't worry. I've got it handled." She ended the video with a thumbs up and a big smile. Hopefully, it was convincing enough that her family and friends wouldn't do a panicked slide into her DMs.

She uploaded the last story, shoved her phone in her pocket, and looked around. No doubt there'd be a premium paid for transportation to Switzerland and beyond. Good thing she had that part already handled. Not that Bossy Blake stuck around long enough to listen. He'd learn soon enough how she'd met a challenge. Train schedules and the German language aside, she was more than capable of figuring out this whole life thing.

In her pocket, her phone notifications went crazy. Startled, she scrambled to free the device and opened Instagram.

Are you okay?

Where's the hot guy you're traveling with?

This is something straight out of a romance novel

HEY. Don't you DARE get yourself killed before my wedding! I mean it!

Leave it to Tina to throw out a threat an entire continent away. Zandra laughed as she sent her friend a response.

But then there were other responses, these from people she'd never heard of. Frowning, she scrolled through her DMs. And there it was. *Flights and Sights* had shared the post of pictures she'd uploaded to their story and tagged her. She switched over to her activity page, and sure enough, she'd jumped up over a hundred followers. And those followers must've been going through her feed, because there were a bunch of new likes on her posts.

Holy crap.

Breathe, Zandra. This is a good thing. More visibility equals more potential jobs.

The thought shifted her momentary anxiety to pride. Her pictures were *good*. Good enough that the travel zine shared them, rather than waiting for the staged pictures she was hired to take.

After assuring a few more people, she replaced her phone and adjusted her backpack just as the next wave of stranded travelers walked past. It was probably time to head back to ground zero—the spot where Blake had left her with growled-out instructions not to move.

As. If. He didn't own her.

The thought had no sooner formed than the man himself climbed the last step onto the platform.

He stopped a few feet away, and Zandra could almost see tension oozing out of him in his stance, in the set line of his jaw. He was a coil of stored energy, and if there was any doubt before, it all crystallized when their gazes locked.

All thoughts of sharing her good news fled in an instant.

They were close enough that she saw the relief and anger and lust blended together in his eyes. It created a vibe so strong it nearly took her breath away.

Then he stalked toward her. And there was no doubt he was stalking. Broad shoulders, long strides, and an intensity in the way he'd slapped his ball cap over his head as he approached. Oh, he meant business, all right. Serious business.

She offered a small smile as he neared. "Hey."

"I thought I told you to stay put." He bit the words out as he scanned her from head to toe.

Yeah, he wasn't exactly happy with her at the moment. "I couldn't get a good connection in there, so I came out here."

"And you didn't bother to call or even text me?"

"I wasn't going to be gone long."

"Didn't it occur to you that I meant it when I said to stay put?" His voice was low, soft, controlled.

Oh God, he was seriously pissed. But it was more than that. She stared at the frown on his face and the tight line of his mouth. But it was his eyes that gave him away. Fear was stamped there as surely as light made all the difference during a photo shoot. It was enough to make Zandra's stomach churn. "Okay, I'm sorry you're so mad, but—"

"I'm not mad, I'm frustrated. Frustrated because I can get two hundred soldiers to follow orders, but I can't get a stubborn blonde-haired, blue-eyed woman to stay in one place." He blew out a breath and gave her a hard stare. "And I'm not sure what to do with you."

"Oh. Well...I had work to do. I had—"

"Let me guess, you just had to get online."

"Hey, there's no reason to mock me," she said, stepping back. "It's part of my job. Not that I'd expect you to understand."

"What I understand, Zandra, is that I'm responsible for you whether you like it or not." He sucked in a deep breath, shaking his head while his gaze never left hers. "I was worried something had happened to you."

He reached a hand out and stepped toward her at the same time, and before Zandra could think about it too hard, she was in his arms, her body pressed against his. Her breath caught as the enormity of the situation crashed with her brain's processing function.

Blake was afraid for her, afraid something had happened to her. Was this a good thing? Did she want it to be a good thing? She'd just found her footing, found her freedom, and here was a guy all over himself worried about her.

Yet through the tumult of emotions that toppled her over and under and back again, the one thought that stood out amongst the rest? Being in Blake Monroe's arms felt as normal as breathing. She closed her eyes and soaked in the scent of his cologne mixed in with a healthy dose of detergent. Who knew laundry soap could smell so sexy?

He pulled back, his hands cupping her face, thumbs lightly caressing her cheeks. Awareness trickled through her, marching into every cell until all she saw was this man, this moment.

"I don't know whether I should kiss you or yell at you."

His soft words flowed through her, kicking her pulse higher. Was he offering her the choice? Because she knew which she preferred.

"If it's all the same to you, I'd prefer a kiss."

He rumbled a laugh and moved closer. "If you change your mind, just say so and I'll stop."

"I don't want you to stop." That was the truth, she realized, mesmerized by his powerful gaze.

The kiss started out soft, slow, as they learned the feel and taste of each other. His lips were firm, inviting, so much so that Zandra tilted her head, angling for more of his taste, more of his touch.

She placed both hands on his T-shirt, the soft fabric covering what she'd suspected, and now knew, was a solid chest, likely chiseled and smoothed from hours of Army-required PT.

His hands were busy, too. One hand traced her hip, the other caressed her face so gently, slowly, methodically as his lips played on hers, teasing them apart and requesting an entry she was only all too happy to give.

His tongue swept in and explored, tasted, dueled for control, and she fought the heady feeling she was diving into an emotional lake and would lose herself in its depths, that she *wanted* to lose herself in it. Time, distance, location… none of it had any meaning in this moment. No, this moment belonged to them. Only them.

Blake groaned and slowly pulled back but didn't let go, his hands stroked her sides before fisting against her jeans.

In slow motion, the world came back into focus, the sounds of footsteps registered… Someone clapped… And heat from the mid-morning sun seeped through her lust-induced fog.

Zandra's eyes flashed open. What was she doing?

His breathing was heavy, as if it had taken every ounce in him to pull away. She could relate.

But before she could say anything, he blinked and stepped back.

"Sorry. That was uncalled for, Zandra." He spiked his fingers through his hair.

Her body screamed at the loss of contact, even as mortification crept up her neck. "Which part?"

"You know which part."

"The part when I chose you kissing me over listening to a lecture about why I should fall in line like one of your soldiers? Because I still believe the kiss was a better option to me."

His jaw tightened. "It wasn't right."

Probably not, but she wasn't telling him that. She cleared her throat and forced herself to focus on the now not-so-empty train platform, the people walking past speaking in a variety of different languages, the beauty of the Swiss Alps in the background... Really, he was doing her a favor, backing off like that. There were so many things to see, and they hadn't even started her work project yet.

"Hey." Blake reached for her shoulders and hunched over to look her in the eyes. "I'm sorry. Really. Are we good?"

She gave a mock sigh. "You've ruined me for any other man, but yeah. We're good." When his hands fell to his sides and his jaw dropped, she laughed. "I'm *kidding*, Blake. Can we get out of here? We need to get to Lucerne and find Madame Pruissard's chocolate shop." The chocolate shop. Her first paid assignment. The reason they were in Switzerland.

"Okay, then." He released her shoulders and straightened, blasting her with a smile that reached across the small space between them. She swallowed past the tide of longing and kept her gaze firmly trained on his, especially since she now knew what his lips tasted like and wouldn't mind another sample.

They headed toward the front of the train station, and Blake pulled out his phone and nodded. "I've got a buddy here who owes me a favor. I can call—"

"No need." She smiled at her foresight. She could do the life thing, regardless of what her parents might think. "I've got it handled."

"Oh?" Blake raised an eyebrow.

"Yeah. I did some research before I left Seattle and found a European start-up company—kinda like Uber, except these are people who are actually headed to the place you want to go. So it's not like they're just driving around wasting gas between rides."

"Like Uber?" He was doing that skeptical raised eyebrow thing again. "Do you mean MOOV?"

Of course he knew about it. "That's the one. It's fairly new, but it's gotten some really great press." She glanced at her phone. "The driver should be here pretty soon."

Once they were outside, Blake crossed his arms, looking sexier than anyone she'd noticed in a very long time. "What vehicle are we looking for?"

"It's kind of hard to tell from the photo. All I see is that it's black." She peered at the screen. "We just have to look for the MOOV flag on the dash. And the driver will text me when he gets close." She pulled her phone out and stared at the screen. "Looks like Moe is on his way." She held her hand up to shield her face as she surveyed the street. "I texted that we'd be by the curb, so I guess we should head that way."

Blake swept his hand in front of him. "After you."

"You're going to let me be in charge?"

"This is your show, and I believe you said you've got it handled, so I'm just along for the ride."

"Gee, thanks." It was about time he trusted her. She

stared at the moving blue dot on her screen as it approached where they were standing. "He's here." She looked up and studied the line of cars headed toward them, most turning before reaching the street that wound its way to the train station's main entrance. For a small town, there sure was a lot of traffic.

She pointed her phone at the approaching vehicles and started recording. "Our MOOV driver's almost here, and then we'll be on our way to Lucerne and my first photo shoot."

She glanced up as a fire-engine red car approached the intersection, then continued through it. "I'm glad it wasn't that one. Seemed kind of small. Has anyone else noticed how small most European cars are? I'm hoping we get something a little bigger."

She turned the phone to Blake. "Wave to Instagram."

He gave an uneasy smile and managed a wave. Well, at least it was something.

"Oh, here comes another car," she said, panning the phone back to the roadway. The approaching vehicle was black and big and...

Wait...was that...

She frowned and looked up from the phone screen as the vehicle crossed the intersection toward the station, flicked its lights three times, and pulled to a stop in front of her. It certainly was bigger than the other cars. Wider, too—and for good reason.

Their ride was a freaking *hearse*.

Beside her, Blake's deep chuckle turned into a cough.

On the dash was MOOV's distinctive blue and white logo. The driver stepped out of the car, a short, stocky man with a huge grin on his face. "Are you Zandra York?" the driver politely asked in heavily accented English.

Half of her wanted to lie, but it was hard to do with Blake snickering beside her. At least she didn't have the camera pointed in her direction, because she probably looked as shocked as she felt. "I am," she finally said.

Blake nudged her. "If you don't post this, I'll steal your phone and do it myself."

She lowered her phone and glared at him. Would it be appropriate to punch your brother's best friend less than five minutes after he gave you arguably the best kiss of your life?

If not, it should be.

Chapter Eleven

Blake really shouldn't tease her, but damn, this was just too good to let pass. He leaned toward her side of the backseat. "Nice ride."

Zandra shot him *the look* and glared. "Shut up or I'll record you snoring tonight and post *that*."

Was that supposed to be a threat? "You gonna post that epic approach or not?"

"I don't know," she admitted after a brief hesitation. "This wasn't exactly what I'd expected."

"Not what you expected. Imagine that," he mused. "Frankly, I'm surprised you got in this thing."

She stuck her nose in the air. "Hey, I have an important assignment, and I'll do what I have to do to get there in time. Even if it means catching a ride in…in…this…" She waved at the space around them.

"Well, good for you." He had to hand it to her. When the hearse had first pulled up, he half wondered if she'd break down in tears. "I read somewhere that MOOV vehicles ranged from farm tractors pulling a trailer to high-end limousines and everything in between, so you never knew what's headed your way."

"I guess I was pulling for a limo." She glanced uncomfortably at the space behind them.

"It's empty."

"I know. I just…this wasn't quite what I was expecting."

"We've already established that."

"You don't have to be so smug." She pointed her phone at him and snapped a picture.

"What are you doing?"

She tapped on the screen a bunch of times then showed him the picture she'd taken. "Congratulations. You're on Instagram again."

He frowned. "What did you plaster on my face? It looks like someone barfing."

"It is." She slanted her eyes at him. "You're enjoying this ride way more than you should."

"And this is a bad thing? I'm trying to be supportive."

"Oh, please. We both know better than that."

He laughed, mainly because he wasn't sure how else he was supposed to respond to her obvious displeasure. Or maybe because he knew what he wanted to do instead.

His gaze dropped to her mouth, to the way her tongue swept against her lower lip as she concentrated on her phone. He'd been so relieved when he'd found her back at the train station, he'd wanted to hold her against him and remind himself that she was fine, even though she looked fine. That she'd told him she'd wanted him to kiss her? Well, that was a no-brainer.

But what did it mean, exactly, that she'd asked for the kiss? Was she interested in him as more than her tour guide? Did she maybe want to use her tongue on—

He blinked. What the fuck was he thinking? He wasn't back in high school, for God's sake, trying to score with some girl. This was Zandra.

Zandra who's tongue was doing the lower lip sweep again as she continued to poke at her phone screen. Clearly she'd blown off the kiss already.

He needed to do the same. Mainly because the kiss had felt too damn good, and he wouldn't mind seeing where it would lead. That was a problem.

He sucked in a calming breath, glad for the space between them, lest he reach for her. Making out in public was one thing, making out in a hearse would be flat-out weird.

She took a deep breath and blew it out. "I'm going to post it. I want my stories to be fun, real, and taking life in stride. This is definitely that."

"Yep. You have to admit it's pretty funny." He chuckled.

"I guess so," she finally said then smiled and shook her head, blonde tendrils escaping from her ponytail. "It's just that there's more riding on this than I expected," she grumbled. "I used to only be sharing things with my family and friends, but I'm starting to get more followers now that *Flights and Sights* re-posted some of my pictures from this trip."

"That's great, right?" When she nodded, he smiled. "So why would you want to change things up? If they're following you, it must be because they like what you're doing. Why add stress trying to change things? Why not just enjoy it?"

She tilted her head, and the corners of her kissable mouth turned up. "Is that what you do? Don't get stressed and just enjoy what you've got going on?"

"Not always." He shrugged. "After all, life isn't always going to cooperate, and sometimes it's just seriously messed up. But I try to use stressful situations to my advantage, try to use them to motivate me toward what I want. Otherwise I don't think straight and end up making shitty choices."

That was part of the reason he had to keep his eye on the future, which meant settling down and going after his law degree.

"Is that why everything you do is planned out?"

"Not everything." He paused. "I'm here, aren't I?"

"Good point." Zandra drummed her fingers on her lap, tapped her toes, and glanced at the MOOV map on her cell phone screen, looking like she was uncomfortable in her own skin.

"Staring at the map won't get us there any sooner," he pointed out.

"What? Don't you believe in mind over matter?"

Clearly what she needed was a distraction. Otherwise there was a chance Blake would be stuck trying to calm her down long before they got to the chocolate shop.

"You know what always works for me? Thinking about my life plan." If he didn't, he ran the risk of being one pissed-off soldier because he was helping his mother instead of chasing his own dreams. "There are lots of times I have to remind myself to be patient, but it's always there in the back of my mind."

"Oh, yeah?" She arched an eyebrow. "You don't seem like the type to have a life plan."

Somehow, coming from Zandra, that bristled. "Well, I do."

She frowned. "I thought you were career military."

"Yeah, well...surprise. I'm just waiting until my mom's done with med school."

"What does one have to do with the other?"

"Said the girl whose parents have more than enough money to put their kids through college."

She grimaced and nodded her head. "You're helping her."

"So is Lily. Mom made a lot of sacrifices to raise us, so we figure it's her turn to reach for her dreams."

"Before you've even reached for yours." She stared at him, frown lines briefly appearing before a slow smile spread across her face. "You're taking care of her."

Yeah…not exactly the direction Blake had expected the conversation to go. He shifted in his seat and stretched his legs out. "The point is, I know when the time will be right for me to do my thing, but until then, I roll with life."

"Roll with life."

"Yep. I convince myself that wherever I am is exactly where I want to be in that moment." It was one of the ways that kept him sane, kept him from being too cagey and anxious to get on with life already.

"What if it's not?"

"Doesn't matter. It keeps me balanced so that, if it isn't really where I want to be, then I'm calm enough to come up with a way to get myself out of the situation and into something better." He nodded at her. "What about you?"

"Well, what keeps me balanced is keeping my word."

"Why?" He hadn't meant to ask the question, only her statement had come out with enough force that it piqued his curiosity.

"You're going to laugh."

"I promise I won't."

She glanced out at the passing scenery. "It's all Santa's fault."

Santa's fault? She had to be kidding. "Excuse me?"

"I never did get the Princess Jasmine doll, and he promised me. When I sat on his lap and told him, he promised me it would be underneath the tree on Christmas morning."

"Excuse me?" he said again. "You still remember that? And you're holding it against Santa?"

"You would, too, if every other girl in your class got one for Christmas and you got an abacus." She sighed and shook her head. "Santa left a note that said an abacus was far more practical than playing with a doll."

Holy shit, she was serious. Blake scrubbed a hand over

his face and tried his damnedest not to laugh. After all, he'd *promised* he wouldn't, and now would be a lousy time to go back on his word.

"My parents have always been like that, you know. Giving me what they think I need instead of what I want," she said absently. "That's why it's always been important to me to keep my promises." She hauled in a deep breath. "And I promised myself that if I ever got the chance to take photographs, I'd do whatever I had to do to make it work." She stared at her phone again.

He had to admire her for keeping her word even when it was very clear she didn't want to deal with it at all. "Yeah, well, for what it's worth, we're in a mode of transportation, and we're in Switzerland, so who the hell cares how we get to Lucerne?" He pointed out the mountain range in the distance. "See the Swiss Alps?"

"You know something? You're right. We're in freakin' Switzerland, and those are the Swiss Alps." She pulled out her camera and started snapping pictures through the window.

"There you go." He grinned at her enthusiasm as she switched back to taking pictures on her phone. The girl was something else.

He leaned back in his seat. The hearse thing didn't bother him. Few things did, truth be told, and there was something to be said for detachment from the things that didn't matter. In his experience, that meant most things didn't matter. It was one of the many ways he'd been able to get this far in life.

Sure, he sometimes wished things could be different, but he also recognized that he wouldn't be half the person he was today if he'd had the stellar upbringing some of his friends had had. Not that he begrudged any of them their good fortune, of course. He was patiently putting the pieces of his life together and making his own good fortune. That was all.

He blinked. Whoa. That was pretty deep shit for someone

on a sort-of vacation.

"Okay," Zandra said. "I did it. I posted the hearse video, a pic of the Alps, and your mug. Keeping it real. Being myself." She licked her bottom lip and smiled. "No stressing."

"No stressing." Blake studied her, at the soft lips he didn't get nearly enough time to explore back at the train station. No, kissing her wasn't a mistake. But now that he'd had a taste, would he be able to keep her at arm's length?

He sure as hell hoped so.

Chapter Twelve

Zandra took a long whiff as she stepped into the crowded chocolate shop. "This whole place smells delicious."

Then again, it was chocolate, so how could it be bad?

"You are the American?" asked an older woman from behind the counter.

Ohmigod. The woman was the quintessential grandmother, complete with a frilly apron over a floral dress, wire-rimmed glasses, and her gray hair up in a bun. Zandra gripped her camera tighter and fought the urge to snap a picture.

Blake gently urged her forward. "You're blocking the crowd," he whispered.

She turned to see a group of tourists waiting behind him and blinked. Holy crap, this place was popular. "No wonder *Flights and Sights* wanted me here," she murmured, moving off to the side.

"The one to take the photos?" the older woman continued as she wiped her hands on her apron and rounded the counter to the front of the store. "Alexandra York?"

Zandra scrunched her nose at her formal name. "Just Zandra." She smiled and straightened her shoulders. Okay, this was it.

"Welcome." The older woman nodded with a broad smile. "I am Madame Pruissard. Let me show you around the shop and then we decide what you will photograph, yes?"

Zandra couldn't help it—she started snapping photos of everything around her as she followed the chocolatier. The petite woman didn't exactly fit Zandra's vision of what the hottest chocolatier in the area should look like. Although she honestly wasn't sure what she expected. A white chef's hat? Starched white apron? Someone more formal?

Didn't matter. Madame Pruissard was billed as the best in the area according to *Flights and Sights,* and the entire shop was utterly charming. They'd passed chocolate flowers, an empty chocolate box with an assortment of foil-wrapped chocolate squares spilling out of it, and an adorable display of a bassinet filled with chocolate baby bottles.

They carefully made their way around the shop, dodging customers with their baskets laden with all manner of items. Madame Pruissard led them past a display of chocolate stars that were hung from a string and appeared to twinkle. The whole place was a chocolate wonderland.

"I don't think I could work here," she told the older woman. "I'd eat chocolate all the time."

"Chocolate is good for you," Blake said from behind her.

"How would you know? You don't eat stuff like that."

"I read it in a magazine." He winked. "It has medicinal properties."

"Don't you mean it's an aphrodisiac?"

He raised an eyebrow, but the corner of his mouth twitched like he was fighting a smile.

"He is right," Madame Pruissard said, interrupting Zandra's thoughts as she followed the older woman's lead toward a corner of the shop. "Chocolate is good for you."

"Yeah, well, I'm pretty sure I could convince myself of that, and that would be the problem. It wouldn't be long before I could no longer fit in my clothes."

"I promise you have nothing to worry about. Now," she indicated the display with a turn of her wrist, "this is my, how do you say? Work in progress?"

Zandra looked past the older woman and stared. Oh, wow. It was a village with some of the structures displayed in charming detail, including a church with its ornate, bejeweled steeple, dusted in gold.

Her gaze traveled over what looked like the town square surrounded by trees, with benches located in various areas around it. Beyond the square was the town itself, quaint buildings with old-fashioned store fronts, its street lined with cars. "Wow. This is all done in chocolate?" She snapped a few more photos.

"Yes. What I could manage, anyway. The rest..." She shrugged. "Well, I will have to have someone make the molds when the time comes."

"They seem too pretty to eat," Zandra said.

"Chocolate should always be eaten," Blake said from behind her. "It goes with everything." He stood a respectful distance away, but she'd swear she felt his heat. The kind of heat that could melt chocolate so it could be smeared on...

Whoa. Smeared chocolate had nothing to do with what she was trying to accomplish here. Her job meant keeping her head, not giving head. Although she'd bet chocolate would go with that, too.

"Yes, of course," Madame said, sweeping her arms wide like a diva giving a personal backstage tour. "Chocolate should always be enjoyed. In fact, every chocolatier has recipes for different kinds of chocolates. Like a chef."

Yeah, well, Zandra wouldn't mind trying a recipe or

two on Blake. She swatted the thought away, shrugged her backpack off her shoulders, and took a determined breath. She had a job to do, and she needed to stay focused here. "It's time to set up. Can we start with this display?"

"If you like. Now, what can I do to help?" Madame Pruissard clasped her hands and beamed. "This will be a fun time."

Yeah, it would. It wasn't a surprise to Zandra that it started out slow. Set up was everything, and that included testing the shutter speed with different shots and angles then viewing them on her laptop. It was the only way she felt certain that the photos she took were any good, especially when coming back wasn't an option. While she mostly liked to shoot from her gut, these were too important to leave to chance.

But even while it took a lot of time, the next couple of hours flew by as she concentrated on each shot, making sure what extra lighting she had to add didn't affect the temperature enough to destroy the chocolate displays. Thank God for modern technology and Photoshop.

From the village pieces to an arrangement of hand-painted chocolate flowers, to the chocolate jewelry made for a little girl's princess birthday party, it was easy to identify the artistic talent that went into each piece. Clearly, Madame Pruissard had earned her title.

All the while Blake stood off to the side, taking cues from her when it was time to move on to another display or carry an extension cord or even hold her laptop while she took the shot.

The whole place was amazing, but what captured Zandra's attention most was the chocolate waterfall the older woman had created. Even now it was surrounded by store patrons eager to dip their purchased cookies, cakes, and fruit into the pool at the bottom of the waterfall.

"This is like one of those chocolate fountains," Blake said as he set up her stand off to one side.

"Only so much better."

"How so?"

"She's taken the trouble to stage it so that it's more intriguing, inviting to anyone who walks by."

"Huh."

"I mean, look at it." Zandra pointed. "There's the chocolate forest that surrounds it, complete with animals that look like they're drinking out of the pool. Anyone would be drawn to this." She swept a hand out. "Look at all these people. They could've purchased a bunch of chocolate, gone home and melted it, yet here they are, dipping fruit and marshmallows and cookies into the lake or holding it under the waterfall—"

"Chocolate fountain."

"Whatever. That, my friend, is the hook that gets them into the shop every time."

He raised an eyebrow. "People travel from all around to drink from the chocolate fountain? Doesn't make sense to me."

"The point is, Madame Pruissard has created something special here. She's displaying her talent, and those who frequent the shop enjoy her chocolate and the experience as a whole. That's all I'm saying."

He studied the display. "Frankly, I'm surprised by your willpower. I'd have thought you'd have caved by now."

"I thought I'd wait until we finished with the shoot." She tilted her head toward the display. "But I think I will. This morning's croissant seems like a long time ago."

"Then go ahead." He frowned. "Although I'm not entirely sure sugar is the best thing on an empty stomach."

"There you go with your 'eat only whole foods' thing. You're on vacation. Loosen up already. Although how you could eat so much so early in the day is beyond me."

He shrugged. "I'm a growing boy." A corner of his mouth turned up, filling Zandra's thoughts with all sorts of inappropriate images. Inappropriate at the moment, anyway.

"Yeah, well, I'm trying some."

"Yes," the chocolatier said, rejoining them. She held out a tray filled with an assortment of cookies, small pieces of cake, fruit, and just about everything Zandra could imagine. "Please, help yourself to a snack while I bring the items out for the next shot, yes?" she said.

"Twist my arm." Zandra forked a strawberry and caught Madame Pruissard's quizzical eye. "It's a figure of speech," she assured the chocolatier. "I promise I'm not asking you to do it."

"Oh, you Americans and your sayings." She grinned. "It is very amusing."

Zandra held the strawberry directly underneath the stream, watching the chocolate layer itself onto the plump fruit. "Are you seriously not having any?" she asked Blake. "I mean, some would argue that the best chocolates come from Switzerland, and guess where we are?"

He shot her an arched brow and chose a cookie from the tray. "Of course I'll have some. Be crazy not to."

Zandra's first bite was amazing. The tartness of the strawberry mingled with the sweet chocolate and partied in her mouth. She closed her eyes and concentrated on the flavors. It was decadent and indulgent and one step below orgasmic. At least, what she remembered about orgasms. It'd clearly been too long since she'd engaged in that particular indulgence.

"Yum," she finally said when she opened her eyes and caught Blake staring at her mouth like he was glued to a particularly riveting show. Her senses tuned in to him as their earlier kiss flooded her senses—his clean scent, the way he possessively held her tight, and the taste of coffee and cinnamon as they explored each other.

She stuffed the longing back and sucked in a deep breath as she tore her gaze away. "This reminds me of romantic evenings and moonlight over a lake, or the ocean, or even a pool."

His eyebrow shot up. "You got all that from one bite?"

"Yeah, well, chocolate tends to bring out the romantic in me. What did you think?" she asked, raising her chin at the half-eaten cookie in his hand. "Any good?"

"Very. But obviously nothing like the...ummm... experience you had."

"Now you're making fun of me."

"Of course I am." He grinned. "That's why I'm here."

See, this easy-going vibe she could handle, and really it made the most sense, didn't it? Instead of kissing him?

Zandra ignored the part of her brain that protested the thought, finished off the rest of the strawberry, and forked up another. She held the fruit underneath the flowing chocolate stream. "One more, then it's back to work."

"Slave driver," he teased.

"Am I?" The question wasn't a serious one, but more to keep the banter going. She enjoyed their exchanges, silly or otherwise. When his face sobered, she was half afraid she might've been pushing him harder than she'd thought.

"You're one of the hardest working people I know, Zandra. You push to get the right shot—whether it's the angle you're standing at or the lighting or the way the shot looks on your laptop. I've never seen anyone work a camera the way you do."

"And how many photographers do you hang with?" she asked, even as she felt her face flush with the compliment.

"That's not the point. The point is, if anyone is a slave-driver, it's you, all right, but you drive *yourself* pretty hard."

He cocked his head to one side. "Have you thought of becoming a soldier? We could use someone like you."

"Very funny, wiseass."

"Oh, there you go with the language again." He popped the rest of the cookie in his mouth and wiped his hands on his jeans.

"Seriously, photography's important to me," she admitted. "It's how I see the world, and I want to share that." How could she explain it so he'd understand?

"Besides," she continued, motioning with her hands a bit, "how else do I make my dreams come true? How else do I carve the kind of life I want for myself unless I push myself to be better? To do better?" She made a sweeping gesture, chocolate-covered strawberry in hand...then *plop*. The fruit landed at her feet, almost as if taunting her for not eating fast enough.

"Oh, damn it." She stared down at the blob of chocolate that was now smeared across the front of her white T-shirt. Her *favorite* white shirt which now sported a splotch of brown. She couldn't have hit it more dead center if she'd tried.

"Here."

She took the napkin Blake handed her. "How could I have been so clumsy?" she muttered, dabbing at the chocolate, trying to soak up as much of it as she could. "Where's Madame Pruissard?" She looked around the shop, grateful that the crowd had died down enough so she could get the chocolatier's attention.

"I'm going to need to get some water on it," she explained. "Is there a bathroom I could use?"

"The kitchen." She motioned toward the back of the shop.

"Watch my gear, would you?" she said to Blake. "I won't be long."

Zandra followed the older woman, trying her best not to

smudge the chocolate so it didn't leave a bigger splotch.

"The kitchen is through those doors," Madame Pruissard said. She glanced at the front of the shop and the band of Asian tourists who entered. "I must go back and help Bernadette," she said. "You will be okay?"

"Yes, of course." She gave the woman a warm smile. "Thank you for your help. Truly," she said before pushing her way through the swing door.

Ugh. Of all the things to have happened now. Light filled the room from the overhead lighting above, flooding the room so every tool, every box, every bowl could be easily identified.

Her gaze searched past the racks of chocolates, past the worktable set off to one side, to the sink beyond and the row of windows above it. It was quaint, cozy, and so very much like Madame Pruissard, right down to the gauzy curtains. Zandra would have to make sure she photographed the area where the magic took place.

And then she stopped mid-track as her gaze fell on trays of chocolate placed on the large, wood island. These weren't just any chocolate. She swallowed as she took in the wide range of chocolate penises. All shapes and sizes of them. Some even had hard veins running through them, leaving nothing to the imagination whatsoever.

"Holy shit." Her eyes widened even more. Did she just step into a sex shop?

Chapter Thirteen

At the sound of the swinging doors opening, Zandra turned. There stood the prim and proper Madame Pruissard, her white hair in a tight bun and a pair of old-fashioned glasses propped on her nose. All she needed was a habit, and she could've passed for Sister Mary Catherine, Zandra's third grade teacher.

The older woman hurried toward her. "Did you get it out? I have a bit of vinegar that we can use if there still appears to be a stain. Chocolate can be hard to remove, you know."

Chocolate? Oh, right. The reason Zandra was in the kitchen in the first place. "Ummm...I was a little bit distracted." She indicated the countertops. "What are these?"

Madame Pruissard raised an eyebrow. "You mean to tell me you don't recognize them?"

"Well, yeah, of course I do." Heat crept up Zandra's face. She wasn't a prude, for heaven's sake. What was wrong with her? "I just meant, what are these doing here? They're... interesting." Oh, good grief. What was she, twelve? "I mean, I didn't see any of these in the cases, and, let's face it, these are kinda hard to forget."

"These were ordered last week." The older woman's smile broadened. "They are not in front because we often have young children in the shop."

That made sense. The chocolatier was clearly talented enough to make chocolate towns and a replica of the Eiffel Tower, surely something like a penis was a piece of cake for her. "But I don't get it. You make all those gorgeous dioramas out there. Out of chocolate."

"I do." She stepped closer. "But these"—she indicated the molds—"these are special. For the ladies."

Wow. Clearly the older, demure woman who created gorgeous chocolate villages and chocolate jewelry for a little girl's birthday party also had a wild side.

Madame tilted her head to one side. "You disapprove?"

"Of course not." Not now that Zandra was over the shock. "I think they're great." She leaned forward to study a particularly large one that had what looked like a white stream flowing from the tip. "They're very...ummm...life-like."

"Indeed. That is what my client requested, and that's what I attempted to do."

"Do you get a lot of orders?"

Madame shrugged. "Women in the surrounding towns, they know where to come for such items."

"I'll bet."

"I have customers who like to serve these at their events."

"I don't suppose you'd want to share who they are?" If Zandra could nail a photo shoot with one of them, it might be something that *Flights and Sights* would pay extra for.

The older woman shook her head. "I'm sorry. I cannot say."

"Well, would you mind if I took photos of these?" At the older woman's hesitation, Zandra added, "I promise they'll be tasteful, and I'd showcase the wide range of talent you have—from the complexity of something like the Eiffel Tower to the simplicity of a man's penis."

She nearly tripped over the word, not wanting to say it, but what the hell? If a woman like Madame Pruissard could turn these out, Zandra 2.0 could say penis with her head held high.

• • •

Blake hadn't been in too many chocolate shops in his life. He'd had no reason. He looked around the room now and studied the steady stream of customers—mostly tourists with their cameras and selfie-sticks, with an occasional local thrown in. The locals were easy to spot. They breezed in and either went up to the counter and were handed a box of chocolates they'd ordered ahead of time or quickly cruised through the shop. The tourists, on the other hand, lingered.

He tapped on the table that held Zandra's laptop. On the screen was a shot of Madame Pruissard, her gray hair formed into a bun atop her head making her look almost regal. Yeah, the older woman was certainly talented, but there was something in the way Zandra had framed the shot that somehow showed wisdom and grace as well.

He frowned and glanced at his watch. Madame Pruissard had gone to check on Zandra ten minutes ago. Were chocolate stains all that hard to remove?

He caught the attention of an employee and signaled for her to watch their gear before he headed toward the swinging doors to the kitchen.

Conversation stopped as soon as he entered. That's weird. Something was definitely off. The older woman stood to one side, Zandra next to her, and both had somewhat guilty expressions on their faces.

"Am I interrupting something?" Because it sure as hell looked like it.

The women turned to each other, and Zandra shrugged. "I'm okay with it."

"Okay with what?" he asked, stepping farther into the room.

"Please," the older woman said, motioning him forward. "Please join us."

Did he want to? The intensity in the room was palpable, and as he reached them, Blake understood why. His gaze landed on a large, almost life-sized chocolate replica of a man's dick, veins on it looking like they were going to burst, and complete with a stream of white chocolate cum running down the side. Holy shit.

He stopped a couple feet away and his gaze landed on tray after tray of dicks—every size and shape. Not that he was all that familiar with another guy's junk, but given the chocolatier's demand for perfection, he wouldn't be surprised if they represented every size and shape.

"Did you want to try a piece?" Zandra asked. Only then did he notice the knife in her hand. "I can cut some off for you."

"Uhhh…" His gaze snapped to Madame Pruissard and he blinked. "What happened to the grandmotherly-type woman who made artistic chocolate?" The question was out before he could stop himself.

"Does a grandmotherly-type woman, as you say, not know anything about sex? Is that how you would portray such a woman? Because if so, I promise that grandmothers became grandmothers because they have a good idea about a man's penis."

He stared at her, at the amusement in the curve of her lips and the light in her eyes. "Well, I didn't mean it like that," he insisted. What exactly did he mean? And did he even want to go there?

"You are surprised," Madame Pruissard observed. She tapped her chin and continued, "Most young people are. But, you know, we older ones, we know more than you want to believe. Sex doesn't stop because you grow older. Sometimes it gets even better."

Okay, this was a totally weird conversation. Blake glanced at Zandra, saw the amusement reflected on her face. "Help me out here," he said.

"Nope. You're on your own, buddy." She grinned and folded her arms, the dark chocolate stain between her breasts taunting him like a neon light at his favorite Seattle bar. Stupid stain.

"In any case," Madame Pruissard said, "the male anatomy is not something I want to broadcast. It could damage my reputation as an artist."

"Or broaden it," Zandra said. "Think of how much more work you'd receive if visitors to the area knew they could come into your shop and take home a box of these. Just think of it," she coaxed. "You could showcase your wide range of talents, from innocent to naughty."

"Zandra, it's like trying to convince your grandmother to peddle sex. Even if it is just chocolates." What the hell was she thinking?

"And there's something wrong with that? Believe me, if my grandmother was this talented, I'd encourage her to go for it. Why should she let her age stop her from doing what she wanted? Especially if she was talented enough to pull it off?"

Yeah, he probably shouldn't be a part of this conversation. He shifted uncomfortably from one foot to the other.

The older woman chuckled. "I suppose it would truly shock my family to see these in a magazine." She clapped her hands. "That is the best reason of all."

"So, you'll agree to it? I can photograph these?" No mistaking the thread of hope in Zandra's voice.

"Oh, very well."

"Great." Zandra grinned. "Let's get started."

A few minutes later, Blake found himself standing uncomfortably next to Zandra as she grabbed a pair of tongs. Yeah…if there was any way to artfully arrange a plate of chocolate penises, she'd find it.

Even now he was surprised Madame Pruissard had agreed to add these to the photo shoot. The older woman had certainly hesitated long enough. Then again, Zandra had given her every logical reason to use them in the shoot, hadn't she?

Which was part of the reason Blake knew she was good at her job, with her attention to detail and unwillingness to take an initial "no" for an answer. "Good work back there, by the way."

"Hmmm?" she murmured, not taking her eyes off the plate.

"Getting Madame Pruissard to agree to this."

"Oh, right. Thanks."

"You can be pretty stubborn when you've set your mind on something."

"I prefer to think of it as determined."

"Of course you do."

Blake smiled to himself as he watched her nudge a chocolate penis with the side of the tongs. "And a perfectionist, too."

"Blame my parents for that one."

"Oh?"

"Yeah. My parents insisted that I do things 'right the first time' for as far back as I can remember. Do you know what it's like to organize your closet by type of clothing and color?"

"You're kidding," he said, remembering her clothes

strewn from one end of the hotel room to the other—in less than twenty-four hours. "But you're such a slob."

"Thanks." She grinned. "Anyway, by the time I started college, the expectations were pretty clear—which typically meant I was drilled with accounting scenarios every time I came home. All to make sure my work was perfect. After all, I'd be dealing with clients at their company, so that meant I *had* to be perfect." She stood back and regarded her work. "Not that there was any pressure, of course."

"There's no pressure now, you know. With the chocolates," he added at her puzzled expression. "Chocolates are pretty hard to mess up."

"Yes, but getting the right shot does require how the subject is staged. There," she said as she straightened. "Much better."

"It is?" Too bad, because he sure enjoyed looking at her ass when she bent over. "Maybe you should move it off to the left a tad." He tried to stop the grin from his face but failed miserably.

"Very funny." The corner of her mouth twitched up like she was fighting a grin, too. "It's perfect."

He certainly wouldn't argue. No doubt about it, Blake was an idiot. He shouldn't be thinking stuff like that where Zandra was concerned. Even if she did have what looked like a firm, tight ass underneath jeans that hugged every delectable curve.

"Okay." He turned then shook his head to clear it. He was here to do a job. Be her assistant, get her coffee, hold a light, whatever she needed. What she clearly did not need was him staring at her ass, let alone wanting to touch it.

"It could be worse, I suppose," he said, not about to let it go. "You could have to make arrangements to get us transportation again. If a hearse showed up last time, there's a fairly good chance we'd have to ride in a cart pulled by a bicycle or something."

"Very funny." Zandra's gaze bore into his. Without breaking eye contact, she reached toward the plate and pulled off a chocolate penis then held it in front of her. "Look," she said then promptly snapped it in half.

Blake shifted uncomfortably. She looked like she'd enjoyed that entirely too much.

"Oh, darn, it broke." She grinned then bit off a tip.

"Was that supposed to be a threat of some sort?" Blake asked. "Kind of mobster-style or something?"

"You take it however you want. Just quit messing with me." She took another bite of chocolate, the unmistakable snap sending a clear message.

"Got it."

Blake knew they were just kidding each other, volleying words across the space between them. But just in case, he was sleeping with his hands over his balls tonight.

Chapter Fourteen

Blake glanced at the message on his phone. "Stefan's about two hours away," he told Zandra. His Swiss contact, a NATO officer who he'd served with, hadn't asked any questions when Blake had called in the favor. It was one of the reasons he'd enjoyed his stint training NATO officers a few months ago. The contacts he'd made came in handy on occasions like this.

"I can't believe the trains still aren't running," she said, adjusting her backpack.

"No telling when the tracks will be fixed."

"It just wasn't what I'd expected." She blew out a deep breath.

"True, but how about we take advantage of the situation instead?"

"You're right, I know. I was just hoping to edit some of the shots from today." She squared her shoulders. "But there's plenty of time to grab some lunch."

They strolled along the edge of Lake Lucerne, where the water slapped against the concrete boardwalk, its rhythmic sounds a contrast to car engines, honking horns, and tourists chatting in various languages that created a cacophony around them.

He glanced at his travel companion. Excitement seemed to pour out of her, lighting her eyes when she turned to him with a grin. "I still can't believe I'm here. Zandra version 2.0 is on her way."

"Why do you call it that? It sounds weird—like you're reconstructing yourself when there's nothing wrong with you."

"That's just what I've been calling it. You know, since I left my *practical* job and took on this roll-of-the-dice one. Go ahead," she continued with a nod of her head. "Say it."

"Say what?"

"That you think it was a dumb idea, that I should do photography as a hobby and not try to feed myself with it, that most photographers, like authors, don't make enough to pay for basic expenses, let alone be able to eat off their work. Go ahead. Believe me, I've heard it all from my parents."

"Wow. Defensive much?"

"Sorry," she breathed out a moment later. "I guess maybe I am a bit touchy about it."

"Well, for the record, I don't think that anymore."

"Anymore?"

Did he really want to get into it with Zandra? Honesty couldn't hurt. "I might've wondered why someone who was handed a huge leg up in life would walk away from it. But now..." He shook his head. "I don't think that at all."

She shot him a sideways glance like she didn't quite believe him.

"It's true. I was watching you there." He thumbed the direction to the chocolate shop. "You're very passionate about your work, and it's clear that photography is in your heart. And that's the life path you need to be on, not some accounting job that sucks your soul." He looked around them. "Where are we going again?"

"Food. I'm hungry."

"That's what I thought, except you walked right past two restaurants without stopping."

"Oh, well." She pointed at one side of the lake. "I want to walk across Chapel Bridge first."

The long, covered bridge beckoned, its original fourteenth-century woodwork destroyed by a twentieth-century fire and rebuilt shortly thereafter.

A motorcycle roared past, its slick chrome and shiny black metal a sharp contrast to the old bridge. "We can do that," he said once the bike was a block away.

The bridge crossed over one side of Lake Lucerne and into one end of Petite France with its assortment of restaurants and hotels. Blake had visited the area once while on a long weekend but had taken the shorter pedestrian bridge that paralleled it farther inland.

Back then, he was more fascinated by the defensive wall that surrounded the city. Too bad there wasn't enough time to walk it like he had before. The views of the Swiss Alps, with Lucerne in the foreground, were gorgeous.

"Let's go," Zandra said, indicating the light had changed.

They crossed with the other pedestrians and headed toward Chapel Bridge, beckoning like a light from the past and now crawling with tourists from all over the world, holding selfie-sticks and wide grins. It was the kind of scene Blake usually avoided, but there was something about experiencing this with Zandra that was almost...fun.

Before long, she had her camera out and pointed toward the Swiss Alps. "Majestic," she breathed out, her voice barely audible.

He swallowed, and his heart lurched. She was so damned beautiful...

"Look at the swans," she said, excitedly pointing to

a pair that floated on the surface of the lake. "Aren't they gorgeous?" She tilted her head to one side as she aimed her camera, exposing the side of her neck in a way that made him want to lean over and kiss it. Which was a crazily dizzying idea.

She caught his gaze. "Did you know that a swan will mate for life?"

Uh-oh. The walls shot up, thick and heavy as steel. Maybe it shouldn't have, but Blake was used to a woman drawing conclusions from a first date. Not that this was a first date, or any kind of date, for that matter.

Shit. He needed to quit with the overthinking already. "That's news to me."

"It's true." She placed her elbows on the bridge rail, gazed out across the lake toward the surrounding Swiss Alps, while the lake cut into Lucerne and continued inland behind them. She sighed. "It's so romantic."

She dipped her head until she rested her chin on her hands. He wanted to reach out and touch her, maybe even gather her into his arms and hold her a moment...or twelve.

The ache was so strong, he shoved his hands into the pockets of his jeans to stop himself. "Why are you telling me this?"

"No reason." She turned just enough to capture his gaze. "Just an interesting factoid." Then she raised her head and faced him, leaning a hip against the low bridge wall, her camera hanging from a strap around her neck. "Don't tell me you've got some sort of a hang-up against swans or something."

He shrugged. "Haven't even given it a thought."

She tilted her head to one side and adjusted her backpack. "Well, for what it's worth, I'm just making conversation."

Probably true. It was also probably true that he was just being an overreactive asshole.

He trailed behind her as they walked in silence and admired the triangular panels adjoined to the slatted ceiling and painted with scenes of Lucerne's history. All the while he snuck a peek in her direction, at the sway of her hips in jeans that hugged, at her profile when she stopped to snap a photo, at the sexy flick of her tongue.

There was something about Zandra now that made her so damned fascinating, like he had to fight the urge to be around her, like he had to continuously remind himself not to get too close, too emotionally attached, which he'd never had to do with any other woman before. Ever.

Had to be jet lag. That was the only logical explanation. Except Blake didn't feel tired. On the contrary, he felt... energized. Getting up after a few hours rest was more than enough to carry him through the day and until they got back to Stuttgart tonight.

"Look at the architecture," she said, pointing at the row of hotels and restaurants that lined Petite France. "Amazing. Switzerland is amazing."

She sighed and glanced toward the umbrella-lined tables filled with patrons. "The people, the stores, the restaurants... it's all amazing." Then she stopped and caught his gaze. "Thank you for coming with me, Blake. I know you'd rather be back in Seattle, but I'm glad Jackson talked you into taking his place."

What the hell should he say to that? A whole host of possibilities came to mind, all of them sappy, so he simply nodded. "Of course."

They stopped outside a restaurant, smells wafting out and inviting passersby to open the door and waltz through to an amazing meal. "Not here," Zandra said after studying the posted menu.

"Why not? Looks pretty good." Although, honestly, he wasn't a picky eater. Hadn't ever been as far as he could remember. He hadn't had that luxury.

"Too expensive."

Well, if that was all... "I'll buy."

"Nope. We can do better."

"Wow. You really are serious about this whole venture, aren't you? The saving money part and all."

"It means that much to me, so yeah, I guess you could say that."

"Even if someone else offers to foot the bill?"

"*Especially* if someone else offers to foot the bill." She slowed down until they walked side by side. "Don't get me wrong, I love a good meal—"

"I could tell that last night. You practically licked the plate."

"—but it's sustenance, which pretty much means that if it's edible, then I'm in."

Wow. This was new. Most of the women he dated insisted on candlelit dinners at some fancy place like one of Seattle's many restaurants on the water, or at least overlooking it.

"How about here?"

They stopped in front of a chocolate shop. "Weren't we just at a chocolate shop? You know, the one with the"—he lowered his voice and leaned toward her—"naughty male parts?"

"You mean like the one I bit off?" A corner of her kissable mouth tipped up in a smile.

"You would have to mention that." He stopped himself from putting his hands over his dick. "I figured you'd have gotten tired of the smell by now."

"This one has regular food, too." She held out her phone and the app that displayed a menu. "See?"

"You're trusting another app? After the whole MOOV thing?"

"Hey, the hearse got us here, didn't it? Besides, what

are the chances this place will be bad? There's a line out the door."

"Good point."

She pulled him by the arm. "C'mon, let's check it out."

A few minutes later, they left, packages in hand, and he'd done little more than nod at her animated choices. They sat at the edge of the lake and dangled sneaker-clad feet over the water.

Blake shrugged off his backpack and looped an arm through it. "So you'd rather eat sandwiches while sitting on cold concrete with tourists walking behind us than eat in the relative quiet of a restaurant?"

"It's a nice day out, and we're surrounded by the Swiss Alps. Why would we want to eat indoors?"

"Good point."

"Besides, these are more than just sandwiches," she continued as she handed him a package. "Freshly baked French bread filled with paté and cold cuts and marinated vegetables? I dare say this will be better than anything else we could choose at the moment."

"I'm just surprised you wouldn't want anything more... exotic."

"Blake." She leaned toward him. "This *is* exotic." She swept an arm out. "And this view is unbelievably stunning. If I wasn't starving, I'd be taking some photos now."

"Considering you're wearing your camera like an oversize necklace, I think you're pretty much ready to go."

"Exactly." She smiled. "I believe in being prepared."

"Yeah? Like the Boy Scout motto?"

"I prefer to think of it as my motto." She cleared her throat and pulled the wrapper off her sandwich. "Zandra 2.0 is prepared for any...eventuality..."

Blake raised an eyebrow. "Casual or otherwise?"

She caught his gaze. "Any eventuality," she repeated.

He fought the grin, but it was really tough. Damn, he liked her. Really, really liked her.

Okay, so what was wrong with just riding this thing out, seeing where it went? After all, they were adults. So, yeah, Jackson was his best bud, but that didn't mean he had to know everything. And even if Jackson approved, whatever happened couldn't go very far. Blake had his eye on settling down in a quiet Seattle neighborhood, something that wasn't in Zandra's plan.

He was a smart guy. At least, he liked to think so. Hanging out with Zandra wasn't something he'd done much of when he was in Seattle, and it wasn't likely anything he'd do much of it when they returned. As long as he remembered to keep her in the friend zone, he was good.

"I wish Mom and Dad could see this," she said. "They'd love the view. Too bad they'd never get on a plane to begin with."

"Why is that? They've got the resources, owning their own business and all."

"My mom's a fatalist—the sky is always on the verge of falling, so she spends all her time in protection mode. Doesn't matter what it is, she's looking at all the ways something bad could happen, even if the statistical probability is small." She grabbed her water bottle and twisted the cap off. "It's a wonder she ever let Jackson or me leave the house."

No kidding.

"But eventually, Jackson wore her down with all the stuff he'd pulled as a kid. So much so that when he decided to join the Army, she relented." Zandra's face twisted briefly. "And then all the attention was on me."

"Sounds like things are rough between you and them," he observed, biting into his sandwich.

"Not really. I mean, I love them and all, but they seem to make it their job to drive me nuts."

"Yeah?"

"Yeah." She nodded. "Believe me, I know where the term 'helicopter parents' comes from—my mom and dad seemed to buzz around from the time I could count until...well, now."

"I knew they kinda hovered when you were younger, but now? Aren't you being a bit overly dramatic?"

"Well, technically, they'd hovered up until three weeks ago, when I finally put my foot down."

Three weeks ago. When she'd announced she was leaving the family's accounting business and taking the job with the e-zine. Somehow, Blake could only applaud Zandra for taking a huge leap of faith in herself.

"Good for you for going after your dreams." He held his water bottle out in a toast. "Here's to making them come true."

Chapter Fifteen

That's exactly what Zandra was doing, wasn't it? Making her dreams come true.

So why did the thought of spending this time with Blake seem like so much more than that? Her body tingled in all the right places and then some, hyperaware of every look, every touch, every word he said like he'd hung the moon. Great. She was apparently living the consequences of having kissed him.

But she still had a job to do.

She stared at the snow-capped Swiss Alps in the distance. "The thing is, it's completely unfair, the way they'd set up different rules for me and Jackson. It's irritating, the way he got to do what he wanted while they pretty much micromanaged my life."

She chewed thoughtfully as light bounced off of the lake, and she leaned forward, mesmerized by the way it played over the relative stillness of the water. Maybe she could frame it well enough from where she was sitting. She'd removed her backpack when they'd sat down for lunch, the bag secured between them, one arm looped around a strap in much the same way Blake had done with his backpack.

If she angled herself to the left, she just might— "Hey," she said as Blake grabbed her arm and pulled her toward him. She stared into his eyes, and her heart stumbled. "You have gold flecks." She swallowed. "Mixed in with the brown."

"What?" He sounded as breathless as she felt, her awareness honed to his touch, electric tingles spiking through her from the point where skin met skin.

"Your eyes. They're beautiful."

He threw her a lopsided grin. "Isn't that my line?"

"I didn't realize that it was gender-specific."

He released her and slowly pulled back, creating space between them, space her body objected to. "I just didn't want you to fall in."

She blinked. There it was. Someone else thinking she couldn't take care of herself. Zandra huffed out a breath and sat upright, even as her heart hammered and the heat from his arm seared her beneath her shirt. "You know, it's not like a girl can't take care of herself."

"Consider it my version of self-preservation. You're right about this, by the way. It's very tasty," he said, biting into his sandwich again.

"Self-preservation?"

"Yeah." He swallowed then smiled. "I don't want to have to dive in after you if you fall in."

She sniffed in mock hurt. "I wouldn't fall in, and even if I did, I promise I can take care of myself."

"Uh-huh. As proven by the hearse that brought us to the photo shoot."

"Will you let that drop already?" She grinned. "I got over it. It took a little while, but I finally did. Besides, riding in a hearse before my time was a small price to pay to get where I want to go."

He tore off a piece of bread and tossed it at a pair of swans then quickly tossed another to the one who didn't get it. "My mom says stuff like that, too, whenever she's got a paper to write or has a lab to finish up that she's not feeling too good about. She says that it's a small price to pay for her to get to be a doctor one day."

"A doctor, huh? I think that's cool." Why hadn't Blake been on her radar before? Oh, sure, she'd noticed him, had thought he was cute, even, but now she found herself intensely interested in all things Blake. She blinked at the realization. Yeah, he was cute. So what? She had enough self-control to not let it get out of hand. Maybe.

"Yeah. She started a couple of years ago. Believe me, it hasn't been easy. A lot of her life hasn't been easy."

Blake wasn't the kind of guy to just spill his guts. That he would willingly do so... Something important was happening here.

"She sounds pretty special." What else could one say to something so...intimately shared?

"After my grandfather died, my sister and I used to trade off making meals because Mom had to sometimes work late and barely had enough time to come home and change before heading off to her next job. Only, Lily was so bad at it, I finally gave up teaching her what I knew and just took over making dinner myself."

So that's how he'd learned how to cook. "Judging from last night's frittata, you've had a lot of practice in the kitchen."

"I used to watch the cooking channel. There was a chef who had a show about the science behind the food. Let's just say it gave me enough of the basics to be able to throw some sort of a meal together with whatever my mom had available."

He cocked his head to one side. "I took care of Lily because she was too young to take care of herself. And, really, how fair was it to expect a ten-year-old to make dinner? She could barely handle a knife properly."

Well, that was one way of looking at it.

Blake tore off another piece of his sandwich and tossed it at a stray cat that had wandered as close as it dared. The animal snatched it and promptly ran off.

"Do you always take care of everyone?"

He stared off into the distance and seemed to consider that for a moment. "Maybe. I don't know. Never really thought about it."

But, of course, he did take care of everyone around him. She'd seen first hand how he'd helped the old lady at the train station, at the way he'd continuously, annoyingly, looked after Zandra, and now, it didn't surprise her that he'd throw a piece of his food to stray animals.

Really, the more she thought about it, there were layers to Blake Monroe that she wanted to peel back and explore.

But if she were a smart woman—and she was—she'd leave things alone, take her photographs for the e-zine, then beat feet back to Seattle as quickly as she could.

At least, that was the plan. Now all she had to do was execute it.

• • •

Blake glanced around the limousine, Zandra seated next to him with her arm looped through the backpack beside her. She apparently heeded his instructions, not letting her guard down even in an enclosed vehicle. Didn't take long for her to create a habit, which he supposed was a good thing, even if it did seem a little weird at the moment.

He settled in and grinned. "Nice ride."

Across from them, Stefan Meier shrugged and handed Zandra a glass of champagne. "Helps me get around."

It wasn't a surprise the guy was chill. All through the

NATO Special Forces classes they'd taught together through the years, Stefan took his job seriously but never took himself too seriously. It was enough to gain the admiration and respect of the soldiers, including Blake.

Stefan reached for a decanter. "You still drink that God-awful bourbon, Blake?"

"Why? You got some in this fancy Barbie-car?" he asked, smirking at his friend. "'Cause it looks like married life has softened you up over the years."

Stefan snorted and handed him a glass. "You're just mad because I'm smarter than you, better looking, and luckier."

"Luckier?" Zandra asked, her head tilted to one side.

"Yeah. Lucky enough to have met an incredible woman." Stefan sighed.

Shit. The guy was soft, all right. What kind of a guy mooned over a woman like she was heaven on Earth? Especially one who'd pulled him from a brilliant career at NATO?

Zandra's smile reached across the small space and made him wish for one moment that they had the limo to themselves. "That's really sweet. She's obviously very special."

"Oh, she is. Thanks to her, I have all this." He spread his arms wide.

"There you go, downplaying the situation again," Blake said. He knew the time and energy that Stefan had put into starting and building his business over the last five years.

"It's true," Stefan insisted. "If not for her, I wouldn't have left NATO and started my own cyber security firm. I am so thankful that I even met her."

"Then I guess all this is thanks to me, seeing as how I helped with that introduction." He winked and took a sip of the bourbon, enjoying the slow burn that came with it. "Although maybe I'm the one who should've met Anna first."

Stefan chuckled. "That, my friend, is what you get when

you play wing-man and also why you are godfather to the twins."

Now that was something Blake could get behind.

Stefan turned his attention to Zandra. "Tell me, how did you get mixed up with this guy? He's an asshole."

"Tell me something I don't know," Zandra teased, jabbing Blake in the ribs with her elbow. "I got stuck with him."

"You sure it isn't the other way around?" Blake asked mildly. Truth be told, it was kinda cool that Zandra got along with his buddy so well. Not every woman did. Then again, it wasn't like he typically introduced a woman to his friends, either. Things usually got dicey, and he hated the drama that came when a woman mistook meeting his friends as a sign they were now officially a couple.

Only this time, he had to admit that the thought wasn't quite so bad.

"Hey," she said with a smile in her eyes. "You're the one who hopped a plane and flew over of your own free will. Don't be blaming me for that."

Stefan chuckled. "See? Already she makes you a better man. She makes you own your shit."

As they laughed together, Blake's gaze slid across the seat toward Zandra. She'd fared pretty well, given the time zone difference. Not that he'd cornered the market on getting by on little sleep. It wasn't any big deal for him, the military saw to it that he could function on what sleep he could get.

But Zandra? Despite the time zone change, the travel, and all the work she'd put in today, she chatted with Stefan like she kept that kind of schedule all the time. "Your children sound adorable." She smiled and tipped her champagne flute in Stefan's direction. "What an amazing family you have."

"I owe my wife for that, too." He blew out a breath and smiled.

Yeah, the guy was toast, all right. Smothered with honey.

It was sickly sweet disgusting. That'd never be Blake. He was far too practical for that.

"Oh?" Zandra leaned forward. "How come?"

That was the thing with Zandra, wasn't it? She liked people, was truly interested in them, and made friends wherever she went. Too bad she didn't work for the State Department. She'd make a damned good diplomat.

"It was because of Anna that I've learned to slow down and see the joy in everyday experiences." He shrugged. "Some say she'd tamed me." He looked pointedly at Blake. "I say she saved my life."

Toast. And there was no saving him.

"Tell me that's not true. If we were alone, I'd remind you of some of the shit you'd pulled," Blake said mildly.

Stefan shrugged. "Doesn't matter what I did before, only where I'm going now."

The guy had a point. He'd left NATO, developed a freaking software app, and now ran his own company. "Judging from the limo, I'd say you're going places."

"And Anna and the boys are with me all the way. That, my friend, is what success is all about."

Only if a guy had that luxury. Not that a family *wasn't* in Blake's plans, but it was way down the list of things he needed to accomplish. He squashed down the pang to his chest. Way down. Third floor basement down.

He shifted in his seat. "I'm glad you're happy."

"As you pointed out, you had a hand in it. And now, by picking you up and delivering you to Zurich, my debt is on its way to being repaid." Stefan glanced at his watch. "It's unfortunate there isn't enough time for you to meet Anna and the twins," he said to Zandra. "But the children are sick. It is why they cannot come with me to Florence tomorrow."

Blake watched as Stefan and Zandra chatted on about Italian food and places to visit like they were old friends.

What would it be like for the four of them to get together one day? Stefan and Anna, Blake and Zandra?

Blake and Zandra.

He had to admit, it had a nice ring to it.

Chapter Sixteen

Late afternoon light glinted off a window at a distant castle. They'd gotten back later than they'd expected last night, so Zandra was glad today's shoot hadn't started until mid-afternoon, with the hotel grounds a short train ride from Stuttgart. Definite plus.

She sat in the front row of VIPs and stared through her camera lens at the woman who swept past on the runway before them, dressed in a gown made from flattened soda cans in a swirl of white and red, and with the beverage's familiar name prominently displayed like a metal breast plate on a female knight. She furiously snapped shot after shot, her shortened tripod in front of her.

Camera in hand, she pulled back, stared at the image on the screen, and worried her lower lip. It looked fine, but no telling what it'd really look like until she saw it on her laptop later tonight. She fought back the mass of nerves that rumbled her stomach.

Breathe. She had to remember to breathe. She was a good photographer. Good enough that *Flights and Sights* had faith in her ability to pull off this assignment, even one where the angle wasn't ideal and the lighting even less so. She'd compensated where she could and would have to depend on a photo app to clean up the rest.

She flicked her gaze back onto the stage. The fashion show hadn't sounded like anything special when she was first told about it, but now she was glad she was here. An annual event, it was open to designers in the towns surrounding Castle Lichtenstein, and the hotel's garden boasted a huge crowd, each of whom had paid several Euros for a seat. There was a fairly good bet that there'd be more visitors once Zandra's piece was published. At least, she hoped so.

Excitement bubbled up inside her, almost completely overriding her nervousness over the photos she'd taken. She could do this. She could affect what happened in a small part of the world just by publishing a few photos. She could change things, change lives. And it felt damned good.

She smiled as the crowd erupted in a round of applause when the designers stepped onto the stage one last time. "That's a wrap," she said.

"Recycling at its best," Blake said as he stood and stretched.

"Are you being snide?" She removed her camera from the tripod and studied the settings. It was time for what she did best—random shots.

"Not at all. I'm amazed what can be done with flip flops and magazine covers and pop can tabs."

"It's kind of like a live version of *Project Runway*," she said, snapping a few photos of the crowd.

"*Project Runway*? I'll have to Google that."

"You've never heard of *Project Runway*? It's a show that features up-and-coming designers who have to produce clothing given a set of parameters," she said. "For instance, on one episode, a designer made a formal gown entirely out of ribbons."

"Sounds...fascinating..."

His face remained neutral, and she rolled her eyes. "I didn't say the show was for everyone."

"No, no, you didn't. Which is a good thing because I'm betting I'd be bored to tears."

"Oh, come on." She nudged him with her elbow. "You have to admit there were lots of creative stuff showcased today." She grinned. "Like the pop can tabs. Who knew they'd make great jewelry pieces?"

He shaded his eyes from the afternoon sun, and when he turned to her, she saw curiosity stamped in them. "Yeah, but I wonder how many women would prefer it to something that comes out of a Tiffany box."

"You might be surprised. If it came from the heart, I'm betting a lot of women would think it very romantic. Besides, recycled stuff is cool."

"I suppose you think it's the mark of our generation, recycling stuff."

"I think it's responsible of us. We shed light on the amount of garbage humanity generates. And when that garbage can be made into something else? Well, that's really cool. Look at the talent, the ingenuity just in this part of the world. This might be an annual, local event, but who's to say it can't catch on and grow into something worldwide one day?"

"You're really into the worldwide thing."

"I like thinking big." It was one of her markers to being successful. She reached for her camera bag. "Who wouldn't?"

"Why?"

That was a curious question, one that made Zandra stop, her hand on the zipper tab as she considered her answer. "Well, I care about people, their cultures, their traditions...I guess what binds people together is what matters to me, and I think most of us want to take care of the planet as best we can, even to the extent of turning our trash into art. It might even inspire others to create something beautiful."

"Inspiring beauty." There was something in the way he said the words that made her pause once more.

God, he was all sorts of yummy with his sunglasses propped on his head and a T-shirt pulled over broad shoulders and tight abs. And then there was the way he looked at her…a lopsided, playful grin that seemed way more inviting than it probably really was.

She mentally shook her head and took the backpack Blake handed over. "Huh. I've never really thought about it before, but I suppose it's why I love photography so much."

"Excuse me?" He shot her a raised eyebrow. "I'm not making the connection."

Of course, he wouldn't. He was too practical, too logical. "I think photography allows me to showcase people and places, celebrating the differences in how we all view the world, view life, but also showing the things that bind us together."

"I see."

She checked the battery on her cell phone. There was still a lot of juice left in it. Good. "You know, despite our differences, at our core, we basically all want the same thing— to live a life we can each consider successful, no matter what metric it is we use to define what success is."

He whistled, long and slow, his mouth puckered so that her imagination went on a wild ride. "That's pretty deep."

She blinked and snapped herself back to reality. "I'll take that as a compliment." It was more than what her parents had offered when she'd shared her passion with them. "I like unique things like the soda tab jewelry we saw today."

"You mean like the turtle-shaped one?"

She nodded. "And the one shaped like a three-dimensional heart? That one's pretty special."

"You like hearts?"

"I'm a girl. Of course I like hearts. And I see it everywhere. I suppose you don't."

"Why would you say that?"

"You're a guy."

"That's sexist."

"Sorry." She looked around her seat as the crowd passed by. The last thing she wanted was to leave something behind.

"You're really not, are you?"

"Not so much."

He laughed, the sound spiking her awareness level even though she'd managed to keep it at bay since they'd dipped a proverbial toe into equally proverbial intimate waters.

Why did she have to react to him like that, anyway? She knew better, but apparently her body had other ideas. Like sex. Stat.

Stupid hormones.

She stood and glanced his direction. "What's so funny?"

"I like your honesty." He grinned, and her heart skipped a beat. "What are you thinking?"

"Nothing good," she muttered.

"Or maybe it is?"

She felt the weight of his stare as she zipped up her backpack. Was there something suggestive in his tone? Nah. She was just imagining it.

"Anyway, this assignment, working for *Flights and Sights*, this is my first step in showcasing all the ways that people are alike, that we're all after the same thing for ourselves and our families."

He whistled, low and soft, the sound trickling through her senses with all sorts of silent promises.

Get a grip, Zandra.

"That's why it's all important to you, isn't it? Getting the perfect shot, from the right angle, the right lighting...all of it."

"Yeah," she admitted. "Although, honestly, I'm no different than anyone else when it comes to perfection with things that are important to me."

"But there's something else, isn't there? I mean, seems to me anybody can mess with lighting and angles, but I saw some of the photos you'd downloaded to your laptop last night, and it's more than any of that. There's a...depth to them. Like a person can *feel* the photo."

She stared. He got her. He really understood what she saw when she focused on her instinct. "I guess I trust my gut and shoot what speaks to me." She raised her camera and aimed it at a particularly colorful hanging basket, its flowers cascading over the side in a fall of bright pinks and oranges, purples and blues. She could almost feel the colors bursting as she snapped a rapid succession of photos.

"Careful." Blake gently grabbed her arm and tugged.

Traces of electric pulses arced through her from where his hand touched her bare skin. She lowered the camera as a little boy ran past with an ice cream cone. "Oh, thanks."

He nodded and let her go, and she ignored the sense of loss. "I didn't think you'd want a repeat of, you know, what happened at the chocolate shop yesterday."

"Right." She blew out a breath and tried for a smile. "Wouldn't want that."

There was something so mesmerizing about his eyes and the flecks of gold in them. Too bad she wasn't Blake's type.

Come to think of it, what was his type anyway? Traveling around as much as he did gave him ample opportunity to meet a variety of women, so—

Wait. She was doing it again, wasn't she? She didn't want anything serious with Blake or any other guy, for that matter. Not that he wanted anything serious. At least, not with her, which was a good thing. He had plans to settle down—

something she didn't want for herself.

She stood beside him, every part of her tuned in to Blake, to the nonchalant way he grabbed his backpack, to the way he readjusted his ball cap, even to the laundry soap smell of him.

Sure, she wasn't ready for a relationship, but that didn't mean she couldn't have a little fun along the way, did it? Maybe even have a little fling?

Zandra glanced at Blake. The thought was tempting. Very tempting.

"We're done for now," she said, adjusting her backpack over one shoulder. "Want to walk around before we head for the train station?"

Blake shrugged on his backpack, too. "Sure."

And just like that, the easygoing vibe was back. Really, it was better this way, wasn't it? Better that they stuck to a more friend-like relationship since that was all they'd be—friends.

Who are you trying to convince? Zandra 2.0 wouldn't care where the relationship ended and would just enjoy the ride.

Yeah, well, Zandra 2.0 would have to be overridden on this one. "I saw some sort of a rock structure in a corner of the hotel garden. Like a monument of some sort." She held up her camera. "I'd like to see about getting a few shots of it."

"Let's go." He stood off to the side, one arm swept wide, and allowed her to pass. "After you," he said, his gaze holding hers.

A shiver of awareness slid through her, as soft and sleek and powerful as the limo that carried them to Zurich last night. Only this time, Zandra wasn't sure where a ride with Blake would lead. And she was pretty sure she didn't really want to go there...pretty sure.

"Thank you," she said. Her voice had lowered an octave, and she saw the moment he realized that, saw the answering flicker in his eyes that drew her closer.

She dropped her gaze to his mouth. One kiss. One harmless kiss…

Trouble was, she knew it'd be anything but harmless. Even now, the memory of yesterday's lip lock was seared into her, filling her mind, her imagination, filling every part of her with a longing so intense she wasn't sure how much more time it'd be before she gave in to the desire she was sure they both wanted.

"You're welcome." He smiled and reached a hand out to the strand of hair that had escaped her ponytail and tucked it behind her ear, his touch delicate against her cheek. Zandra fought the urge to lean into him and stepped back instead, much as her body protested the loss.

She blinked and walked past on thankfully steady feet, even though her heart pounded out a hard, erratic beat, and every part of her longed to turn back and demand he hold her…and more.

She forced her attention to their surroundings. A spattering of sunlight filtered through the trees and onto the ground, creating a cool pattern that moved each time the wind rustled the leaves. A child's distant cry filled the air, interrupting the chatter as fashion show patrons mingled, some leaving the hotel grounds while others sought a courtyard table. Life seemed simpler in this moment, and Zandra was pretty sure she wanted to keep it that way.

"This place is so pretty." She stopped in front of the hotel's restaurant and peeked through the window. "See?" she said, pointing to a display. "A heart. Told you I see them everywhere."

"You're kidding, right? Those are chicken breasts. Probably what they're serving for dinner tonight."

Yeah, he had a point, but still…"They're placed so that they resemble a heart. Can you really not see it?" And did it matter to her one way or the other if he did? "Oh, forget it.

Never mind." Some people had no imagination.

They reached the rock mound with the intricate cross placed on top, its multi-colored stones catching the fading afternoon light.

"Those can't be real jewels," Blake said. "There would be guards around this...thing." He shook the metal fence surrounding it. "This isn't even very sturdy."

"It's still pretty." Zandra pointed at the center of the cross. "I wonder what the inscription says?"

"The placard's faded."

Zandra looked through her camera lens at the cross and the top of a distant church spire that jutted up behind it. That'd make a great shot. "I wish I could capture more detail," she murmured.

"Of a bunch of rocks?"

She did a slow walk around it and took in the wide base. "It's a piece of art." And it was beautiful. Zandra smiled. "Don't you think?"

"You say that about almost everything." Blake shoved a hand through his hair, the longish strands falling in disarray.

"I see art in almost everything." She walked around the monolith and studied it. "With the cross on top and the church spire in the distance, it speaks to the church's determination to conquer something as dead as a rock."

"Seriously?" He raised an eyebrow. "You see all that?"

"That's the story it's telling me." She blew out a breath. "My other lens would've been perfect for this."

Too bad it'd been stolen. She frowned. How could seemingly nice people turn out to be thieves? Worse, how could she have let her guard down and allowed it? Well, she knew better now.

Zandra casually glanced around them. "You know, there's nobody around..."

"They're all at the other end of the garden. Probably

enjoying the after-party."

The rock formation had a flat spot close to the top where, if she stood just right, she might be able to capture the cross and the spire and the ridges of the rock right along with it.

She looked around again. What the hell? It couldn't hurt. Even if the e-zine didn't want the photo, she could probably sell copies herself. *Note to self: create a website to sell my photos.* Not that she was entirely sure how to make that happen, but she'd figure it out.

She dropped her backpack on the ground and climbed over the railing. "Hey," Blake loud-whispered behind her. "What are you doing?"

"What does it look like I'm doing?" She gripped the side of the rock with one hand. "Gloves would be perfect right about now."

"You shouldn't be climbing that."

She stopped to look at him, one sneaker-clad foot poised against the rock. "Why not?"

"Because the sign says so." He thumbed a plaque that had been placed in front of the monument. "No climbing."

"How about that?" She shrugged. "There it is in plain English."

She proceeded to hoist herself up then stopped a couple feet off the ground. "There's no need to get excited. I got this."

"You'll fall and break your head."

"Or maybe I won't." It helped to be optimistic.

"I'm serious, Zandra. Get down."

"Now you sound like my mom."

"That's not an insult. Your mom's pretty smart."

"I don't need your permission, Blake." She shot him a look before focusing on the cross that beckoned like a star in the night sky, only it was far more accessible. "I am so doing this."

Chapter Seventeen

Blake wasn't sure if he admired her determination or not, but at the moment, he sure as hell couldn't stop her, especially when she shot him *The Look*. "Be careful."

There was that look again, like he was an idiot for voicing the obvious. "Hey," he said, climbing over the metal rail that was clearly ineffective at keeping Zandra out. "It's that self-preservation thing. Your brother will kill me if anything happens to you."

Her brother? Hell, his mom would get first shot, and that wouldn't be pretty, either.

"I'll make it quick," she promised.

He felt like a colossal dick as he stood there, watching her ascend the rock, but there was barely enough room for one person, let alone two. He positioned himself right underneath her, arms outstretched. If she fell, maybe he'd have a chance to catch her.

Don't fall, don't fall, don't fall… Sweat trickling down his back, he sent up the silent plea.

Zandra took a step up, then another, her body leaning

forward as she climbed. And all the while, he held his breath. What if she really did fall? And she broke a bone or, worse, broke her neck? He'd never forgive himself.

After what seemed like hours to Blake, she'd finally reached a flat spot and stopped.

"Now what?" he called up to her. "There's not enough room for your tripod. Didn't you say you needed it because it holds the camera steady? How 'bout you just come on back down?" He motioned her down with one hand, which was idiotic, considering she was totally ignoring him.

Blake held his breath as she carefully raised her camera with one hand then let go of the rock she'd been holding. "Don't worry, I've got it."

This was a bad idea. A very bad idea.

She snapped a few shots, brought the camera down enough so she could look at the rock tip again, and began taking more photos.

"Zandra." Damn it. His voice came out as more of a plea than with the firmness he'd planned on. He was a Special Forces officer, for Christ's sake, and while he could instruct a room full of mostly cocky, highly competent soldiers, he couldn't control one determined, feisty female…and it fucking sucked.

"There," she said, replacing the lens cover on her camera. "All done."

Her descent took far less time than the climb up, thank God. It wasn't until she finally stood in front of him, her face smiling up at him and a light in her eyes that Blake finally broke.

He reached for her and gently tugged her forward, wrapping his arms around her. She was safe. And, damn, it felt good to hold her, good to pull her close and know she was back on firm ground again.

"Your heart's racing," she murmured, the camera slung

around her neck pressing against his chest.

"Gee, I wonder why." He retreated just far enough to pull the camera over her head and set it on her backpack beside them. "I swear you took a year off my life."

She swallowed, her gaze dropping briefly to his mouth before flicking up to his eyes again. "I'm sorry."

The warmth from her body warmed him like it was the most natural thing in the world.

Damn it. He'd told himself he wouldn't do it, told himself he'd keep his distance from Zandra because the last thing he'd wanted was for either of them to get carried away.

Yeah, kissing her was a bad idea, no doubt, but still…

Her lips parted, then she raised onto her toes, her hands playing on his chest making Blake smile. Leave it to Zandra to make the decisive move.

He dipped his head down, and the moment she opened underneath his kiss, a weight lifted off his shoulders. This sweetness, this touch, this moment—these were all reserved for Zandra. Nothing else mattered but the feel of her mouth on his, the way her tongue dueled, invited, teased.

He tightened his grip on her hips and gently pulled her closer. Somehow, his brain registered her deep moan, registered the way she moved against him, synchronized almost, and spurring all sorts of thoughts in his head. None of them good, all of them good.

Did it matter, really, what his brain labeled right or wrong when the feel of Zandra against him inspired all sorts of scenarios he likely wouldn't be happy with, either?

She pushed herself up against him, shifted just enough that his erection strained even harder. Was she teasing him? God, he hoped not, but he wasn't about to ask. Better to let things play out, no matter how they played out.

From somewhere a drum beat insistently, and a voice over a mic registered. He groaned. The band was about to kick in.

He pulled back and smiled when she leaned toward him, mewling softly, her mouth searching for his. He couldn't help it. He leaned toward her and planted another kiss on her soft mouth. "This probably isn't the time or place," he said regretfully. Damn, how he wished it were.

Her eyes fluttered open, and she swallowed, nodding. "Yeah, you're probably right." Her tongue snaked out and moistened her lower lip.

"Now you're just teasing," he said.

As if to prove her point, she cleared her throat and took a step back as she tucked a few loose strands of hair behind her ear. "Am not."

Cute ear. Was the area behind it sensitive? If he kissed and licked it, would she respond?

If he were a smart man, he'd steer clear of Zandra.

Although the way he'd been behaving lately, he was beginning to question just how smart he was.

• • •

From what Zandra had seen so far, Cologne was as charming as its inhabitants. They'd finished the shoot at a local teashop where patrons could purchase tea blends or mix their own. The adjoining café even gave them the ability to brew it themselves. The owners were delightful, and the atmosphere light and fun.

Thankfully so.

Since that kiss in Lichtenstein a few days ago, she'd managed to keep her brain focused on work, keeping herself occupied as she combed through the photos she'd taken and retouched those as necessary so they were ready to be submitted to *Flights and Sights*.

She'd been tempted to share some of the photos on social

media, but her editor was right. It was better to hang onto any still shots until it was time to run promotional material.

But now that the shoot was over and they were settled in their overnight extended stay location, Zandra was forced to face facts. Somewhere over the last couple of days, Blake intrigued the hell out of her. Or maybe it was just because it'd been awhile since she'd been with a man. Either way, her attraction to her travel partner was bad. Very. Bad.

Sure, the guy was intelligent and caught on quickly, anticipating what her lighting needs were or offering suggestions on how she could get a better shot. Once or twice she'd had to agree that he was right. He even graciously hauled her stuff around and kept an eye on her backpack if she needed to do something as silly as climb a rock.

Despite all of that, it was annoying. Was there anything the guy couldn't do?

"You mind chopping the carrots?" Blake asked.

Yeah, then there was the fact the guy could cook on top of it all. Really, couldn't she catch a break somewhere along the way? "Sure."

"So, the best way to cook a barbacoa is low and slow," Blake told her. "That way the meat's tender and juicy and tastes even better than what's served at a lot of restaurants, if I do say so myself."

"Uh-huh." She washed her hands. "So how come we're having steak instead of that?"

"No blender, no CrockPot, not enough time."

"All good points," she said, chopping the top off a carrot. "But now it seems like you're just teasing me with how good your barbacoa is."

"I promise to make it for you...one day," he said then shrugged. "Maybe before I PCS out. Jackson might be back by then."

Permanent change of station. Right. Army-speak for

moving to a different base and yet another reason not to get involved with Blake. The Army owned him, and while Zandra didn't know enough about how the Army planned things, if her brother's tour schedules were any indication, a soldier didn't exactly get to choose where he went.

"How'd you and Jackson get to be friends, anyway? All I remember is that one day, you showed up at our house and it's like you've always been around."

He threw her his signature charming grin, and Zandra's heart did this funky skip, the zap of electricity arcing through her like he'd touched her in all the places that craved him.

Bad thought. Very, very bad thought.

Or maybe, actually, a good one?

God, now she was thinking the way he might. Of course, it was a bad thought. Nothing good could come out of any sort of a relationship with Blake that went beyond friendship.

But did it have to go beyond friendship?

The real question was, could she handle a physical relationship with Blake even if she knew it wouldn't amount to anything?

"I'll take that as a good thing."

Startled, she looked up from the last carrot she was slicing into rounds and into his gorgeous brown eyes. "Huh?"

A corner of his mouth quirked up. "How I met Jackson," he reminded her. "You said I just showed up one day and seemed to be around ever since."

"Oh, right." That'd teach her to daydream while in the middle of a conversation. She shrugged, feigning ambivalence. "I didn't notice anything other than you seemed to be around."

"Ouch." He squinted and stopped chopping. "For the record, that's painful for a guy to hear."

"You'll live."

"Barely."

"So, go on," she prompted. "Tell me how you guys became friends."

"It was a dark and stormy night…"

She rolled her eyes. "Jeez. Spare me all the gory details."

"No, really, it was a dark and stormy night. Jackson had just finished football practice, so the two of us were going to grab a bite when he realized he'd lost his car keys. We went back to look for them and had rounded the corner to the football field by the locker rooms. There was this kid, Tom, who was backed up against the wall, with this bully threatening him.

"Seems that Tom came from a wealthy family, and the bully wanted his allowance." Blake shrugged. "Probably didn't help that he bragged about it more than he should've. Anyway, there weren't any adults around, and this kid had a history of getting away with his bullying, so let's just say Jackson and I took matters into our own hands."

"And you ended up in detention for a couple of days. I remember now. My brother refused to tell my parents exactly what'd happened."

"It's a code of honor thing. And for the record, the bully got expelled from school once we pulled all the facts together for the principal." He scraped the carrots off the cutting board and into a bowl. "That's when I finalized my plans to be in a career where I could see that justice was done."

"Wait. Let me guess: you wanted to be a superhero."

"Those who need defending don't need a superhero. They just need enough people to step up and do the right thing." He said it so quietly that she knew this revelation was big. Huge, even…

"This is why you went military," she said.

"Yeah." His gaze held hers, a glint of something in them. "And that's why I'm going to law school, too."

Law school? She raised an eyebrow. What else didn't she

know about him? "What made you decide that? I mean, not that I don't think you can't do it."

He frowned and measured spices into a bowl, his movements slow, methodical, like he was weighing his words as carefully as he spooned the spices. "I knew when I was a kid that I wanted to go to law school. My dad was killed by a couple of thugs, and I knew I wanted to grow up and put the bad guys away, I wanted to protect the world from them."

He'd been through all that as a kid? That he had such depth plucked at something deep inside her.

He grinned, and the mood shifted as he shook his head. "Yeah, well, I don't need to advertise it. Besides, Mom's got a couple more years of med school, then once she's in the residency program, it'll be my turn."

Wow.

Zandra stared.

She was beginning to discover the different facets of Blake Monroe: good friend, patient traveler, caring son, great kisser. Definitely a great kisser.

"So you want to go to law school like my dad did to defend the defenseless?"

Really, it made perfect sense.

"More like I want to see to it that justice is served," Blake replied after a moment. "That kid was scared. He didn't do anything, didn't hurt anyone, yet some bully thought it'd be okay to forcibly take something from him. That's just plain wrong.

"I'm not naive enough to think I can save the world," he added. "But I'm not standing around waiting for someone else to do it, either."

Well, damn. What was she supposed to say so it didn't sound like she was being too mushy? But was he serious about any of it?

The intensity in his eyes was something she'd never seen

before. This belief, this calling he had to bring justice to the world, was it a short-term deal? Given how long it'd been since he'd graduated high school, not likely. No, Blake was committed to protecting those unable to protect themselves.

Damn it to hell and back.

Zandra stared at Blake as he seasoned the steaks. Somehow, some way, he'd managed to chip away at the protective screen around her heart.

Chapter Eighteen

Blake wasn't quite sure what the hell prompted him to spill his guts this time, but there wasn't a damned thing he could do to take it back now. She continued to have this effect on him, and it was unsettling as hell.

Or was it comforting?

He wasn't ready to examine how he felt close enough to decide which one. Not yet.

Thankfully, Zandra hadn't brought it up once they'd sat down to eat, although he'd been more than prepared to shut down the conversation.

Now he glanced across the hotel room kitchen as she walked in, DVD case in hand. "Found something in the hotel library," she said. "I hope it's good."

He cleared his throat as he put away the last of the dinner dishes. "Good or not, all that matters is the translation. Any movie will do. It's what I did to learn different languages wherever I was posted. Would you trust me on this?"

"Okay, fine." She held up the TV remote control. "Honestly, though, I can't tell what it's even about, so I'm telling you right now, if it's a horror movie, I'm out unless you want me sleeping next to you tonight."

He snapped his gaze toward her and caught the moment when her words sank into her brain. A bright shade of pink flushed her cheeks, and she blinked a couple of times. "I mean...ummmm...that is..."

"Yes?" He crossed his arms. "Go on, I'm listening."

"You're making fun of me."

"Yep. And enjoying every second of it." He grinned. "So, what are you going to do about it?"

"How about ignore you? I should probably put this away." She picked up a discarded T-shirt, stood from where she'd been perched on the edge of the blue sofa, and tossed the shirt across the room and onto her bed.

He chuckled. "You're such a rebel. What would your mother say now that you're such a slob?"

She tilted her head and gave him a mock glare and raised her chin. "I'm going to make some popcorn."

Ugh. He hated popcorn, but there was no way she'd know that. Besides, there were worse things in the world than popcorn. He hung a kitchen towel on the oven's handle and turned as she pulled a package out of the cupboard.

"Good thing I went to the store with you or we might not be having this tonight." She opened up one end of the package and slid a bag out.

"Yeah, that would've been a disaster."

"You're mocking me now."

"What was your first clue?"

"Funny guy."

He laughed. "Seriously, we just had dinner. You can't be hungry already."

"I'm not, but what's a movie without popcorn?"

"Ummm...a movie?"

"An incomplete experience."

"Says you."

"Says a lot of people." She pushed some buttons on the microwave. "I'm beginning to get the impression that you don't like popcorn, but that's impossible. Everyone loves popcorn."

"I don't."

She leaned a hip on the counter and regarded him with cool, assessing eyes. "And why not?"

He shrugged. "It's not that big a deal."

She leaned forward as if imparting earth-shattering news. "So humor me."

He crossed his arms and saw the challenge in her eyes. Why the hell not? "When I was a kid, my mom worked more than one job."

"I know. You'd told me. That's when you'd learned to cook."

"Well, you're assuming there was something to cook." When she stared at him blankly, he continued. "She was a single mom with two kids to feed. Sometimes she didn't have enough to get us through the month, so she bought popcorn. Not the kind you stick in the microwave—that kind was too expensive—but the kind you did on the stove. Let's just say I ate a lot of popcorn when I was growing up," he said. "So I don't much care for it now."

Yeah, okay, that was putting it mildly. Truth be told, he hated the taste of popcorn, could barely stand the smell, too, and while he realized his distaste wasn't logical, in a sad way it kind of was.

"Oh." Her eyes widened. "We don't have to have popcorn tonight," she quickly said, turning toward the microwave.

"Don't be silly. Go ahead and have your popcorn. I promise I'm okay with it."

That was a logical response, a way of laying the past to rest and focusing on the future. Did that even make sense?

He wasn't exactly sure, but he'd run with it for now.

She tilted her head to one side and stared at him like she was trying to make up her mind one way or the other.

"Honestly, Zandra, have the popcorn. I promise it won't push me over the edge."

She lifted a shoulder in a shrug that caused her short T-shirt to draw up and reveal a small expanse of skin. "Okay."

"I'm sure you won't be offended if I choose not to have any."

"Of course not."

Blake still pondered the exchange as they sat down to watch the movie a few minutes later, a bowl of popcorn on Zandra's lap. He tended to carefully monitor his words, tended to keep his private life very private, yet in the space of a few days, Zandra seemed to have changed all that…and he didn't feel weird about it, either.

"Ready?" he asked.

She nodded and chewed.

"Are you sure you got enough at dinner? Because you're shoveling the popcorn in pretty good." It was actually nice to be around a woman who wasn't afraid to eat. Even if it *was* popcorn.

She threw a kernel at him. "Hit 'play' already."

The movie started easily enough with a woman at the stove wearing an apron and a pair of high heels. Unfortunately, that was all she was wearing…and then the milkman walked in…

Zandra coughed and scrambled for the remote, nearly spilling the entire contents of the bowl.

He turned his head just far enough to catch her gaze. "Did you honestly not know this was a porn flick when you chose it, or are you trying to seduce me?"

She whipped her gaze toward him, eyes wide. "I can't believe you'd even suggest such a thing." She reached for the DVD box between them. "Does this look like a porn flick to you?"

A woman stood by a stove stirring a pot with a small smile on her face.

"She's fully clothed, as far as I can tell, and there's nothing on the jacket that even remotely suggests it's a porn movie. And for the record, it's not like you offered to go downstairs and pick something out."

"Huh. You have a point. On both counts," he added at the glare she shot him. "I don't suppose you want to keep watching this?"

She stood and walked toward the TV. "Oh, gee, let me think. No."

He chuckled. "Well, put on something else or do you not trust yourself?"

"Keep it up and I'll throw this remote at you."

"You sure are cute when you're trying to be mean."

"Who's trying?" she muttered.

He grinned and leaned back, his feet on the coffee table. This was the kind of relaxing evening he'd imagine sharing with a woman one day. Chilling with a movie on after dinner. The feeling was very...pleasant.

Within a few minutes, she resumed her place next to him. "No subtitles," she observed between bites. "How's your German again?"

He cleared his throat. "I'm good to give it a try." Not that he understood much beyond a few phrases, but she didn't need to know that.

The scene had two men in it, at a bar. Well, that narrowed it down some. "Huh, that's interesting."

Zandra sat up and leaned forward. "What is?"

"That guy, the one on the left, he's a spy."

"He doesn't look like a spy."

"Do you even know what spies look like? They're supposed to blend in wherever they go, assume the part of whatever role they've been assigned. They don't exactly walk around announcing themselves. I'm guessing it has something to do with self-preservation."

"Oh, right. That self-preservation thing again. Good point," she conceded.

He forced his face and tone to remain neutral. "He wants out of the spy business, but his friend there, the one on the left, brings up a good point. Righty wouldn't know what to do if he *wasn't* in the spy business. After all, it's not like there's a market for guys who know how to eavesdrop and sell that information on the black market."

"Actually, there probably is."

"Hey, who's translating here? Me or you?"

"Okay, okay, I'll be quiet." She turned her gaze to the screen. "Now what's he saying?"

"He says he'd only meant to be in it long enough to put his mom through medical school, but then he'd planned to go back to school himself."

"You don't say?" She nodded gravely. "Sounds like he's a really good man."

"Oh, he is. He's the best." Blake raised his chin toward the screen. "That's what his buddy just told him."

"I bet family's important to Righty, too, huh?"

"Yep. Family is all that matters. Doing anything he can to help his mom out, to help his sister out, that's what he lives for."

Damn it, what the fuck was wrong with him? He wasn't normally chatty about his life and generally preferred to live it with his cards held close to his chest. But somehow, tonight, with Zandra, it felt...right.

She chuckled. "You're really something, you know that?"

"Yeah, women tell me that all the time." Unsolicited, at that.

She swatted him across the arm. "Really? I'm trying to

be serious here."

"So am I." He grinned when she laughed out loud. "Is it my fault you don't appreciate what other women do?"

"What I'm trying to say is that you're a really nice man."

"And how do you know that?"

She tilted her head to one side. "Let's just say your movie translation helped me figure it out."

"Oh?"

"Like it wasn't obvious you were talking about yourself." She grinned. "You're a nice man, Blake, so just own it already, okay?"

Could he own it?

God, he wanted to, if for nothing else than to see the light in Zandra's eyes. The problem was that he was so thoroughly screwed, and it somehow didn't matter to him. At. All.

What the actual fuck?

Chapter Nineteen

"What's happening here?"

Zandra hadn't meant to ask the question. Really, she'd figured that if she played her cards right, she'd skate through the next week with Blake and then head for home. Hell, they weren't even on the same flight, so there'd be no awkward airplane good-byes, but maybe a friendly hug at the airport.

At least, that had been the plan, only now…

There was an undercurrent of tension between them, and not the bad kind, either. No, this tension electrified, practically crackled the air around them. Judging by the quiet intensity in Blake's gaze, he wasn't immune to it, either.

"I'm not sure I know," he said. He blew out an audible breath. "This wasn't exactly something I'd counted on."

"Does anyone ever really plan on *this*?" She set the bowl on the coffee table and angled herself so she sat facing him. "Sorry, that's a silly question and completely irrelevant to the conversation." She glanced his way again, the low voices emanating from the television now barely registering along the fringes of awareness.

"You're nervous."

She blinked. "Is it that obvious?"

He nodded. "You clasp your hands together then start fidgeting so your thumbs look like they're chasing each other round and round."

"I do not—" She stared at her clasped hands. "Damn," she said, pulling them apart.

He chuckled and reached for her, his touch warm as she edged closer so only inches separated them. "Look, *this* is a bad idea. You know it, and I know it."

"Yeah, it is." Yet at the same time, *not* pursuing *it* was an even worse idea.

"So how about we play it cool for a bit? No rushing anything, no demands, no...nothing."

"Play it cool." She stared into his eyes then flicked her gaze to his mouth and back. Just one kiss. One delicious, soul deep, panty-melting kiss. She could certainly participate in something like that, then stop. She knew all about boundaries, right? She could take it slow.

"Okay," she said, decision made. "I can do that."

"Can you?" His voice was a whisper away, and he lowered his head slowly, ever so slowly, then stopped just a few short inches away. How could something be so close and still so far? "Even when I want to kiss you?"

"Oh, now you're really testing the limits of my control, aren't you?"

"Builds character."

"Does it?" She tipped the corners of her mouth upward. "What if the tables were turned? What if I did this?"

She leaned forward, closing the gap between them and moving off to one side of his face where she hovered just shy of his mouth.

She was testing him, all right, and she didn't have long to wait. In half a heartbeat, he turned his mouth to hers, captured it in a kiss so intense, so powerful, yet gentle, too.

God, he tasted so good. Like wine and promises.

Blake shifted, pulled her closer to him like he couldn't get close enough. She returned the intensity of his probing mouth, eagerly opening to him, their tongues in a duel for control.

He wanted her. There was no way Zandra could deny that. He said it with his kiss, with every stroke of his hands over her back, her shoulders, her hips. He wanted her, and God help her, she felt the same way.

Could she ever get enough of him? The thought lingered a moment then quickly evaporated as Zandra groaned with each pass of his hands, each caress of his tongue. Her nipples hardened, and the moist spot between her legs wanted more, demanded he do more than just kiss her.

He stopped and pulled back far enough to gaze in her eyes. "Hey." His voice was husky, like it cost him some effort just to speak. "Let's just chill and watch the rest of the movie. What do you say?"

He said the words, and while she believed him, there was a part of her that was touched. He cared enough to stop, cared enough to let her decide which way things would go tonight.

Warmth enveloped her, made her feel...special. There was no other word for it. "Watch the rest of the movie," she echoed. "I don't understand German. Apparently, neither do you, judging from your interpretation."

He grinned. "We can make up our own story."

"Will it have a happy ending? Because I like happy endings."

"So do I, Zandra." He caressed her cheek, his fingers warm against her skin. "So do I."

God, she wanted to believe him. Did she dare?

• • •

Sunlight slanted through a slit in the window curtains and produced an unfortunate beam of light smack dab in the middle of Blake's forehead. He blinked his eyes awake as two things registered. First, he was still fully clothed, stretched out on the couch, and second, Zandra was in his arms and sprawled beside him.

Her head was tucked underneath his shoulder, and she snored so adorably against his chest that it made his breath catch. Her lips parted slightly, bringing all sorts of memories with that tiny movement.

He'd thoroughly kissed that mouth last night, dueled with her tongue, and tasted and tangled and…craved even more. Even now, his dick stirred. But he knew better than to rush into something, for his own sanity as well as hers.

She breathed softly, evenly, like she was totally content with the way her life played out. He wanted to shift enough to study her more, to learn the shape of her eyes, her face, her nose, everything about her, but he didn't dare. Movement meant risking she'd wake, and he didn't want that yet. Not when she'd had several days of travel and work. It only made sense that her schedule would catch up with her now.

Besides, she seemed so relaxed, and she trusted him to keep watch while she slept. A pool of pride kicked up. It was his job, and he was more than okay to do it.

It didn't take a rocket scientist to see what kind of woman Zandra York was on the inside, too. All anyone had to do was be around her for a short while to *feel* the way she cared about life, about her work, about the people she came into contact with.

No doubt about it, she had a very bright future indeed.

A strange pang smacked him on the chest. Her dreams were her own, that's for sure. They had nothing to do with him or her family or any other cause besides wanting to help others see the ties that bind humanity together so that they all could become the best possible version of themselves. And she was happy to travel all over the world to do it, too. So where would that leave him? Leave them?

Zandra mewled softly before she shifted, turning so that she faced Blake fully, both hands on his chest. His throat tightened.

That sensation last night, that sense of rightness in the moment that he'd felt as they'd sat and watched a movie— those feelings paled in comparison to holding her now, to having her trust him enough to fall asleep.

She took a deep breath, and he shut his eyes. The last thing he wanted was to be caught staring. Besides, there was a fairly good chance she'd freak when she woke up, so maybe giving her a moment to process wasn't a half-bad idea.

At least, that was the plan.

Zandra's eyes fluttered open, and she immediately gazed up then smiled. He was still asleep. Good. They'd both needed the rest, given the crazy travel and work schedule they'd kept since arriving in Germany.

She studied the lines of his face and the strength etched into his jaw. She wanted to touch him, wanted to trace a finger over the light stubble on his chin to the swell of his lips that she knew did crazy-wonderful things to hers.

She had one hand on his chest, and she felt the thud of his heart through the thin T-shirt he'd worn last night. They'd fallen asleep, still fully clothed, so why did she feel so deliciously naughty? Like she'd committed some act that she wouldn't have normally done? Although, honestly, it wasn't like she'd slept with many guys and definitely not fully dressed and on the couch or anything.

Yeah, getting involved with each other was a bad idea.

A very bad idea. They both knew that. But where was the harm in just letting things be, in letting life play out with no thoughts of where *this* might lead them?

She froze as Blake opened his eyes, then he glanced down at her. He seemed confused for a brief moment, but it didn't take him very long to recover.

"Hey." He threw her a shy smile then played his free hand through her hair before lowering to trace the curve of her face. "Good morning."

God, he was even more attractive after having just woken up, stubble and all. Awareness tripped through her, made her hyperaware of the way her heart raced, and her brain took all sorts of left turns so that all she could think of was where their tangle of arms and legs would naturally lead.

"Good morning." Zandra felt a slow blush creep up her cheeks along with the touch of nervous energy that skittered along her nerve endings, jolting every cell awake and throwing a party. Whatever happened to her suave, sophisticated version 2.0 self? Clearly she'd been abandoned.

"Sleep well?"

"Yeah." She swallowed, her gaze falling on his mouth. "You?"

"Yeah. The best."

He bent his head down toward hers, and damn if it wasn't like a magnet, drawing her mouth toward his.

Like their previous kisses, this one was soft, gentle, not enough to get carried away, but with their bodies pressed together, it was more than enough to stir some very sexy thoughts in Zandra's brain, thoughts that involved little clothing and a nice, wide bed.

As if he read her mind, Blake pulled back. He chuckled softly.

She skimmed her hand across his chest, loving the solid feel of him against her fingers.

"Hi," he said.

"Hi."

He gave her a shy smile.

Wow. Was it possible that he was truly as unsure about any of this as she was?

"You ready to get the day started?" he asked, caressing her cheek again.

No. She wanted to lay around instead, maybe move to the bed where they'd both be comfortable.

But Zandra knew better. She was here on assignment, a reminder she was tired of hearing, even if she was just talking to herself. She needed to rouse herself out of the comfort of Blake's arms and get on with it. The future waited for no one.

"Yeah," she said, regret lacing her tone no matter how hard she tried to stop it. "That's probably a good idea."

Chapter Twenty

Blake shaded his eyes and stared at the hill with the crumbling remains of an abandoned castle resting on top of it. Today's shoot shouldn't take too long. Thank God.

After this, they had the rest of the afternoon to get back to Cologne and wander through the city before they hit the gallery opening Zandra had wanted to attend. Galleries weren't his thing, but she'd pointed out that there was a better than fair chance she wasn't returning, so of course they had to go.

Yeah, he'd do it. He wouldn't deny her the opportunity, even if it were possible for him to say "no." Because for some odd reason, seeing Zandra smile, watching her eyes light up, these were important to him even though he didn't quite understand why. He sure as hell wasn't going to think too deeply about it, either.

"This is one of the area's hidden treasures," she informed him as they continued their ascent up the slope toward the castle ruins. "A few tourists visit it every year, but it's not very popular."

"Don't you worry that featuring these hidden treasures will somehow ruin them? Make them so popular that tourists tromping through the grounds or visiting the chocolate shop or making the trek to watch the annual fashion show would mean that the local towns would sacrifice the very things that made them charming in the first place?"

She seemed to consider that for a moment. "I'm torn on that point, actually," she admitted. "On the one hand, these events or places are what make the area special, but on the other hand, the extra attention makes it difficult for local townsfolk to keep up with the tourists. There can be added stress just trying to accommodate the throngs of people, although I'm pretty sure the local businesses appreciate the extra foot traffic." She paused. "It's all about growth. Each area has to consider if they can grow with the influx of interest in their event.

"I do make sure to get permission before I shoot, and then a contract is signed to protect *Flights and Sights*. Anything after that, I have no control over."

That made some sort of sense.

Once they reached the top, she spread her arms out and walked toward one side of the ruins, the large stones that once protected the inhabitants reduced to rubble in some places, and the interior opened up to the sky. "Wow. Look at this."

"Looks like a bunch of rocks to me," he said.

She dropped her arms to her sides. "Have you no imagination?"

Oh, he had one hell of an imagination, all right. These days, they seemed to involve a variation of the things he wanted to do with Zandra, starting with pulling her tank top off and—

Dumbass. Heading down that road proved fruitless, even if they hadn't decided what they were going to do with this thing between them. And if he kept it up, there was a good chance he'd end up with nothing but blue balls before they headed back to Seattle.

Zandra pointed to one side of the castle. "This is where the kitchen probably was. The huge fireplace is a dead giveaway."

He watched her face, saw the play of emotions as she quietly moved throughout the large space. "In some ways, you're reliving what might have happened here, aren't you?"

"I suppose. It's kinda fun to make up how people might've lived." She shrugged. "My creative brain likes to entertain me that way. Oh, look." She pointed toward what looked like a turret at one end. "I want a picture."

Blake followed her. It looked like nothing more than a crumbling pile of rock topped with a sharp spear-like structure. "It's a wonder that thing's still standing."

"That's what makes it cool."

He had his own definition of cool, but he was just along for the proverbial ride.

They approached the bottom of the stone stairway, and Zandra lowered the camera. "I can't get a close enough shot." She blew out a breath. "Too bad I don't have my long-range lens. It might've worked."

Uh-oh. "I'm not liking what you're thinking," he said, stepping closer.

"How do you know what I'm thinking?"

"You've got that look on your face—the same one that you had when you climbed that rock back in Lichtenstein. Remember that? It's a wonder you didn't break your neck."

"*Pffft*. You worry too much."

"I'm serious, Zandra." He crossed his arms and stared at her.

"So am I." Her forehead crinkled briefly. "The lighting's perfect this morning. I've got to get closer." She scurried up the first couple of stone steps. "C'mon," she called over one shoulder. "Loosen up a little, would you? We're on another leg of our adventure."

Adventure. Right. "This doesn't look very safe."

She tentatively placed her foot on the next stone step. "Seems fine to me."

"Zandra."

She turned. "What?"

"That doesn't look very stable. You'll fall and break your head open. Or worse."

"Oh, please." She gave him *The Look* before turning away. "That's what you said last time, and everything turned out okay. Besides, there isn't a warning sign or anything."

"Not that that would stop you," he said drily.

"Fine, stay there if you want."

Shit. Clearly, they were doing this. Blake sucked in a deep breath. Maybe she was right. Maybe he needed to loosen up and just enjoy the experience. One thing was for sure, he certainly wasn't going to let her go alone. He placed his foot on the step and tested his weight on it. So far, so good. Then again, he was just inches off the ground.

By the time he got to the top, Zandra had her camera raised and was snapping photos. He knew better than to distract her, but he still kept watch of where she stepped. "One wrong move and you're falling," he warned.

"Yes, Dad."

"I like your dad, so that's not an insult. The man has a lot of sense that obviously didn't transfer down to his daughter." He grinned. "Sticking your tongue out at me isn't an insult, either. In fact, I can think of a few things you might do with that tongue."

"Oh, really?" She lowered her camera, and something shifted, tightened like a cloak wrapped around them against the cool breeze. "And what would that be?"

A corner of his mouth quirked up. "Use your imagination.

I hear it's quite creative." Anything he came up with would be deliciously, torturously slow, too. He gave himself a mental shake. He needed to stay focused or he couldn't help Zandra if things went south. His gut clenched at the thought.

"Touché."

She skimmed the tips of her fingers over the stone like she was reading it somehow, her forehead creased in concentration.

There were so many dimensions to Zandra—playful, serious, focused—but the intensity, the purpose that emanated out of her now had to be one of the biggest turn-ons Blake had ever experienced. He knew that whatever she focused on would get her undivided attention, whether it was arranging a platter of penises or shooting photos or video for Instagram.

She pulled out her phone. "Let's do an IG story," she said, as if reading his mind. "I haven't done one yet today."

"Up here?" He looked at the dubious railing that marked the edge of the landing. "Maybe we should do this on the ground."

"No," she said, waving him off with one hand before tapping the screen on her phone. "It'll be fine."

Damn it. She insisted on posting from up here, where the rail was rickety and the slightest pressure would likely send her plummeting to the ground.

Not on my watch.

Blake planted himself firmly in front of the rail while she panned the view and commented on the history of the place in a reverent voice. He blew out a breath. It'd be better if they did this from below so she wouldn't *be* history with one small step, but it was too late to stop her now.

"Everyone say 'hello' to Blake."

Shit. He hated being in front of the camera. But as soon as he caught Zandra's gaze and stared into her eyes, he felt his face form into an answering smile.

She sure was beautiful, but more than that, she was gorgeous on the inside, too, where it mattered.

Slowly something shifted inside of him, something he was pretty sure he should put firmly back in place and rivet shut. But for the life of him, he didn't want to.

Chapter Twenty-One

Staring into Blake's eyes was…amazing. It was like she could walk in and find peace there.

"Hey, everyone," Blake said, staring at her instead of the phone. "Zandra's right, this place is beautiful."

His words floated over her like the lightest caress and made her heart pick up speed. It was like he'd touched her, and every inch of her being wanted more. Zandra blinked. What the hell was wrong with her?

She turned the phone around and hoped she didn't look like she was forcing a smile. "I gotta run now, but stay tuned and I'll be back soon with more from Europe." She waved as she ended the live video.

Biting down on her lower lip, she turned the phone around and poked at the screen, every cell in her body completely tuned to Blake standing a short distance away. God knew how she managed to concentrate long enough to upload the stories, but thirty seconds later she glanced up, and her heart did a funny flip-flop thing.

Blake sucked in a deep breath and blew it out, his gaze

fixed on hers. Energy oozed out of him like he was the caged lion she'd photographed at an Oregon wildlife preserve, ready to pounce at the slightest provocation. "You ready to go now?"

His words were slow, measured, like the question had a deeper meaning behind it, which was just plain silly. She squashed her overactive imagination. "Yep. Let's go."

Zandra picked her way down the remains of the staircase, careful to be in the middle of each step. She should've been more concerned about the condition of the staircase, that she might take one wrong step and the whole thing would come crumbling down. The old her would've definitely been more concerned, but clearly that woman wasn't around today. Good thing...

"What was so important that you just had to get up there?" Blake asked once they were back on firm ground. "And don't tell me it was for the view."

Zandra tilted her head to one side. "You didn't see?"

"See what?"

"A heart. There was a heart carved onto the side of the turret."

"How could you even see it from down here? How did— wait a minute. You knew that, didn't you? Before we got here?"

She shrugged as they walked toward one end of the castle ruins. "The e-zine gave me a chance to find one place on my own, so I did some research of the area and tried to find a destination that would appeal to travelers on different levels. Not only is this castle off the beaten path, but it's got a romantic history to it. You wanna hear?"

"Do I have a choice?"

"Once upon a time—"

"Very funny."

"Hey, it *was* a long time ago." She cleared her throat.

"There was a dude who wanted to earn the love of a maiden, only her family was stuck up and wouldn't entertain the idea of him being part of the fam. So, he sold his services as a mercenary for several years, saved up his gold, invested it, then finally had enough to build this castle."

"Did he get the girl?"

"Sadly, no. She died of some disease a few years after her family turned him away. So that's why he had stones carved to resemble a heart. It was because of her that he'd wanted to build the castle in the first place." She sighed. Some stories were just too good to not share. "It's so romantic."

"She died," he said flatly. "How could that be romantic?"

"Leave it to a guy to point that out."

"It's obvious, isn't it? He did all that work, made all those sacrifices, and in the end, he didn't get the girl. Seems like a waste of time to me."

"The gesture, Blake. It's the gesture that's romantic. Just because they didn't live happily ever after doesn't mean it wasn't romantic."

"You do realize that's the kind of crazy talk that gets women into trouble in the first place," he muttered, stepping onto the edge of the path that led to the parking lot.

"Oh, I gotta hear this."

"Why do women think romantic gestures have to be so grand? Guys don't get credit for stuff like cleaning up after the dog or taking out the garbage or—"

"—teaching a bully a lesson," Zandra chimed in.

Blake stopped and turned, his gaze catching hers when he peeked over the top of his sunglasses. "I was going to say helping a woman figure out the train schedule, but let's go with that. Present company excluded, of course." He blew out a breath.

Of all the things she'd discovered about Blake on this trip, his willingness to step in and help a fellow human being out had to be the most attractive thing about him. It only enhanced her awareness of him.

She nodded. "Well, what you say is true—guys don't get enough credit for doing the everyday stuff, and that's too bad. After all, most women would just as soon have the guy deal with cleaning up after a dog."

He had that sexy don't-give-a-damn smile on his face. "Well, sure, but would cleaning up after the dog earn him a kiss?"

Her breath caught, and every nerve ending in her body crackled, tuned in to Blake, to the way he stood, almost eye level with her since he was on the downhill slope, and the magnetic pull he seemed to have on her.

How could she have known him since high school and not have *known* him at all? Even after the countless times he'd spent hanging around her childhood home?

That she should want to know him now seemed…fitting. Like a promise long overdue and gratefully filled.

"Zandra?"

She heard her name on his lips, his tone just a breath above the slight wind that blew past and barely cooled her. She felt the heat from the top of her head to the tips of her open-toed sandals, felt the tug and pull toward Blake, toward his own heat. What the hell was happening here?

"I don't know," she finally answered. "Kisses are for special things. Otherwise the guy tends to take them for granted because they come too easily."

A corner of his mouth crooked up in amusement, and his eyes bored into her like he was reading her mind, reading her soul. "I'm glad you feel that way."

She swallowed past the roaring in her ears, past the rush of adrenaline that surged through her, wanting, waiting…for what? What the hell was stopping her from taking what she wanted, what she needed, even if it was only for one night?

Or for the remainder of their trip?

"Are you okay?" Blake stepped closer, concern etched in his eyes, in the lines on his forehead. "You've been running yourself ragged since you landed. Maybe we should head back to the hotel and get some rest."

Oh, she wanted to head back to the hotel, all right, but not for the reasons he thought.

She stared as he hoisted the backpack onto his shoulders. They weren't a couple, would never be a couple. Which was just fine by her. But what if, just this one time, things were different? What if she just truly let go and enjoyed herself? Wouldn't that add to the experience of Zandra 2.0?

Hell, yeah, it would.

Decision made, she cleared her throat. "What if I had something else in mind?"

Chapter Twenty-Two

Breathe, buddy. Just breathe.

Blake reached a hand out to unlock the hotel door with Zandra right behind him, so close he could feel her heat, her energy reaching toward him, reeling him in.

He should play it cool, be the suave, sophisticated lover he wanted to be for her, but damn, his hands were shaking. Fucking shaking so hard he wasn't sure he could get the key in the lock.

Finally.

He shoved the door open and held it back as she swept past.

"You're sure about this, Blake?"

Sure? Was she kidding? He swallowed. "Yes." He eyed her closely and stepped into the room. "Are you? I mean, there's still the gallery show tonight." Even as he uttered the words, he mentally kicked himself. Yeah, it was the right thing to do, to say, but still...

She stepped toward him, and he was drawn to that ghost of a smile on her face that crept into her eyes and camped there. "I think this is more interesting than anything on display at the gallery."

No kidding.

"No complications. No drama. Just this one night," she continued, stepping forward again, slowly closing the distance between them.

"No complications, no drama," he agreed, reaching for her.

The feel of her body against his, her upturned face and the blaze of desire in her eyes. It was even better than waking up with her this morning. He reached both hands out and cupped her face. "I'm going to kiss you now."

Her gaze swept down to his mouth. "God, I hope so."

The kiss started out soft, tentative almost, then a spark lit inside him when she opened her mouth and let him in. Their tongues dueled, danced, explored, a precursor of what was to come. His dick hardened, pressed against the fly of his jeans, and demanded out.

When he broke away, he stared into deep blue eyes that held a thousand promises.

This. This was better than what he'd imagined in his wildest dreams.

It was about damned time.

For all her bravado about claiming her life, finding her way through the world, tearing herself free from what everyone expected, Zandra knew a diversion from that path was just that—a diversion. And right now, this diversion with Blake was what she wanted, what she craved with a force that surpassed nailing the perfect shot or selling her first photograph.

And she wasn't stopping now to figure out why.

Want and need dueled with hesitation, defeated it as he

continued to kiss a delicious trail down her neck, searching, learning, fueling her desire past the point of no return.

She gasped at the sensations pouring through her, and she pulled at his shirt until her fingers felt the warm, hard muscles underneath. Nice abs. Tight abs. The man was perfect.

Blake's groan echoed through her as she trailed her fingers across his stomach, flattened her palms against his chest, and drew the T-shirt up.

He broke the kiss long enough to pull the offending garment off and toss it on the floor…and her breath caught. On his chest was a tattoo of a skull with a mass of swirls and curlicues that seemed to emanate from different points off the skull. The tattoo was so much like the man—hidden, reserved, raw, powerful. She skimmed over it, traced the edges with her fingers. "This is beautiful."

"It's art."

"You didn't strike me as the artsy kind." There was so much about Blake that she didn't know.

"Hope that's not a deal-breaker." He flashed her a grin then pulled her into his arms again.

"Not even close." She leaned forward, kissed and licked a trail up his chest. He was delicious, the light mat of hair on his chest rough against her tongue, the pure masculine scent of him mixed with his spicy cologne. All these were Blake, and she committed every part of it to memory.

She'd spent far too many nights wondering what this moment would be like, touching him, kissing him…having him kiss her.

His kisses reminded her of lazy, sultry breezes that tripped through Puget Sound on a warm summer night of endless possibilities. She tilted her head, allowed him to lick a wet trail to her shoulder, then she mewled when he lingered on *that* spot. "You like that," he murmured against her. "Good."

Zandra wasn't going to be outdone. Not by a long shot.

She reached for his belt. Closer. She needed to get closer. Her hands felt slow, clumsy as she tugged on the leather and undid the buckle. "This is more intense than climbing the castle steps today."

"I don't know. Watching your ass sway in front of my face was definitely intense." He hissed when she brushed against his erection. "On the other hand, this is just painful."

"Then I'm glad we're doing something about it." She slowly pulled the zipper tab down, finally freeing him. Then it was like she couldn't move fast enough, tugging his jeans over lean hips and well-toned legs.

As soon as he stepped out of his jeans, he pulled her to her feet and crushed her mouth to his.

The kiss was demanding, strong, pulling everything from Zandra and spiraling her senses higher. She'd known the attraction was there, felt it often enough in their short time together. She just hadn't realized the torrent of need, of want, of feeling that came with it.

His rough hands pulled her close, and his mouth found hers. Claimed her.

The kiss continued, with each pass, each nip, each tug making her want more. Demand more. Finally breaking the kiss, Blake stepped back. His eyes were dark, daring, and she couldn't help but be drawn to them. "Are you sure this is what you want? Because if it isn't, we stop now."

In answer, she pulled her shirt off then shimmied out of her jeans, kicking her sandals out of the way along with them. Then she straightened, saw the flame of desire in his eyes, in the way he leisurely looked over her nearly naked form.

She swallowed deeply. "I can't stop now. I don't want to."

Without another word, Blake scooped her into his arms. "Then I think we need to get you more comfortable."

He laid her on the bed then followed her down. The kisses continued. Searing kisses that scrambled her brain and made her wonder for one brief moment who she really was: adventurous travel photographer or staid accountant unleashed.

He slid his legs against hers, the move slow, sensual, stoking the hunger inside her. She lifted her hips, rubbed the sweet spot against him.

And still his kisses continued. Down her neck again, the sensations so sweet, so damned hot, she was sure flames would consume her before—

He touched her, then, a soft touch, barely there touch, one that ignited a spark so hot she was sure she would combust. Her nipples peaked under his skillful hands, rough hands that had seen more than their fair share of hard work, hands that helped and hands that now caressed so gently, so reverently, Zandra wasn't sure which way was up or down.

She felt warm, restless, wanting more, needing more. "Blake?"

He skimmed his chin over her bare stomach, the beginning of a beard rough against her skin, yet the flame within her burned brighter, hotter, higher.

"Please," she whimpered. "I can't..."

He chuckled, low and soft, all the while planting those damned, drugging kisses on her as he skimmed his way back to her mouth. "Can't what?" he asked.

"More. Need more."

"Show me."

His mouth ravaged hers, plundered, told her that he, too, wanted her. Needed her.

She wrapped her arms around him, stroked the hard planes of his back, and all the while his hands and his mouth were busy, so deliciously busy.

She'd never thought of herself as particularly sensuous. Sure, she had needs like everyone else, had even had them satisfied, but not like this. Never like this. It was like Blake knew exactly how to touch her, how to stroke his hands over her, how to kiss that perfect spot on her neck all the while he did it, elevating her awareness until all she saw or heard or tasted was him.

The flame that'd been building for days now threatened to erupt. "Blake." She whispered his name as he nipped at her ear lobe then soothed it with his tongue.

"Yes?"

"I want…"

There was that chuckle again. "At least it's better than 'I can't,'" he said. "Tell me, Zandra. Tell me what you want."

Shyness was never one of her problems, but it sure as hell was now.

Then he licked that sweet spot on her neck, the one that made her shiver with want and lift her hips up and grind against him, searching for the hard ridge of his erection. "You still have clothes on," she murmured against his shoulder. "I want to fix that." She licked and kissed a trail to his mouth, wanting to give as good as she got, and was rewarded with a groan.

"Slow down." His voice was hoarse, strained.

She grinned against his corded neck. It was her turn to ask questions. "Why? Don't you like it when I do this?" She kissed his jawline, found her way to his mouth.

His tongue immediately swept inside her mouth. She didn't know about him, but kissing him was bliss, heaven, like she'd found her way to a hidden oasis and wanted to stay.

Finally, he pulled back and his eyes mirrored her own desire. "I want to savor every sweet second with you."

Those simple words touched her to a depth she wasn't sure existed, let alone experienced. She shouldn't have been surprised. This *was* Blake, after all.

He leaned back on one bent arm, and his large hand glided over her once more, this time like he was seeing her, really seeing her. He traced a finger around one nipple, and her heart stuttered. "Red's a good color on you." He dipped his head and kissed the space between her breasts, the move so pure, so erotic, it made her heart ache. "Matches your personality."

"I'll remember that," she gasped when he flicked a thumb over her nipple.

He unhooked the front clasp and pushed the fabric aside, and his nostrils flared as he studied her briefly. "Tell me, is your other bud just as hard?"

She frowned. "You're looking at them both. Can't you tell?"

"I meant the one between your legs. The one I intend to get a closer look at before we're through tonight."

"Oh." Jeez. For a woman who claimed to know what she wanted, she felt out of sorts, discombobulated. The pulse between her legs intensified. "Well, in that case, you're going to have to see for yourself." She shamelessly reached between them and pulled her panties off. "There," she said, tossing them aside.

Blake grinned then dipped his head to kiss the valley between her breasts. "Not so fast. Tonight, I'm taking my time with you."

When had a guy ever taken the time with her? Not that those encounters weren't good, but they sure didn't hold a candle to what she felt now, didn't rival the deep, rolling feeling she'd melt under the gaze of his brown eyes, wasn't sure she didn't want to. After all, Zandra 2.0 was open to any adventure, and Blake was certainly an adventure.

He grinned, and the moment he dipped his head and closed his mouth over one hard nipple, she mewled. "Blake."

The sensations were overwhelming, amazing her with the force of their intensity rolling through her and rocking her to the core. It was like pleasure and need drugged her, made her want more, need more. And yet he held back, took his time teasing her, taking her higher.

Zandra groaned, cool air touching the wet spot he'd left behind as he lavished her other breast with the same treatment. She arched her back when he pulled away again.

"Just let go, Zandra. Don't think. Just feel." The whispered words soothed her and made her ache at the same time. This was the dichotomy that was Blake, wasn't it? The wanting and not wanting, the need to stay mixed with the impulse to run.

He continued, the sounds of the air conditioner soon fading so the only thing that mattered was this man, this moment, and the delicious way his hands lightly traveled over her body. And then he quickly skimmed those mind-drugging kisses down her body until he reached that place between her legs that ached for him. She spread her legs wider, raised her hips, and shamelessly offered herself up. The old her wouldn't have dreamed of such a thing, would've been too self-conscious or embarrassed, even.

Thank God that woman was gone.

At the first touch of his mouth on her clit, she reached both hands out and gripped the bedsheets. She groaned, every part of her concentrating on the way he expertly licked and nipped and sucked, the sensations flaming through her.

He continued to tease and torment, so much so that when he pulled back and she saw the deep desire in his eyes, she knew that she was more than ready. She knew she was his.

He raised himself onto his knees, a condom in hand. She'd been so distracted she wasn't sure when he'd gotten one, but it sure didn't matter now. He quickly sheathed himself then settled between her legs again.

"Let me." Zandra reached out and guided him to her opening. She shut her eyes as he plunged deeply, then gasped.

"Zandra. Baby..." His voice was hoarse, barely

controlled. "I'm close."

"So am I," she whispered, her hands holding onto his very firm ass and drawing him closer. They moved in rhythm, the tension building higher, reaching further. Her senses crackled with the intensity, every nerve ending tuned to this man, this moment, until release came in a burst of colors as she plunged into the abyss, Blake following closely behind her.

Chapter Twenty-Three

Talk about mind-blowing sex. He was going to fucking hyperventilate, Blake was sure of it. He sucked in a deep breath, held it, then blew it out slowly, willing his heartbeat to quit racing like he was running from the devil himself.

Some part of his brain kicked in, and he braced his weight on his forearms. Below him, Zandra's breathing had slowed, evened out. He grinned as her eyes opened and a lazy smile crossed her face.

"Welcome back." He kissed the tip of her nose.

"Mmmm..." She tightened her legs around him and stretched. "That was amazing."

"I agree." He chuckled, and a soft pang struck him in his chest, something he'd never felt before with any other woman.

His eyes widened as he took in the sleepy grin she shot his way.

Holy shit. He'd just banged his best friend's sister.

What the hell was he thinking?

"Hey," she said, reaching up a hand to smooth over his forehead. "No regrets, no drama, remember?"

That's right. Because that's what they'd agreed to, and what happened between them was their business.

He nodded. "No regrets, no drama." They were two healthy adults with healthy sexual appetites. That's all it was.

Even though it felt like a whole hell of a lot more.

• • •

Blake walked alongside Zandra past the thousands of locks securely fastened onto the rails of Cologne's Lock Bridge. Why anyone would feel the need to leave a lock on a bridge was beyond him. And as far as tourist attractions went, this wasn't a stop he'd ever felt he'd want to make, and yet here he was. Somehow, it was important to him to do stuff that Zandra wanted, important to him to see her smile and know he was a part of it.

Zandra quickly walked ahead then turned, camera in hand. "Smile," she directed as she looked through it and began snapping pictures.

"I'm guessing shots of me won't do much to advance your photojournalism career."

With each step he took, she moved backward. "Don't be silly. I'm taking practice shots."

Practice. Was that all he was to her?

He swatted the annoying thought away. He didn't want it to be anything else. He had plans. Big plans. Plans that didn't involve traipsing all over the world for the rest of his life. There was no room for a sassy, just-found-her-purpose-traveling-the-world woman like Zandra. And he certainly wouldn't ask her—or any woman—to walk away from her dreams.

Shit. He was overthinking. *Get your head on straight, Monroe.*

Zandra stopped, yanking his focus back to reality. She

was all smiles as she pulled out her phone. "Want to go live with me?"

He narrowed his eyes. "You know I don't much care for social media."

"Yeah, yeah." She waved him off. "It's important to take it seriously and build on that progress."

Focus like that he understood. And she was focused in much the same way he was about his career track.

But was that all he wanted? Would it, in the end, be enough to make him happy?

He quelled the thought as Zandra shrugged, the slight movement somehow inviting, though she likely didn't intend it to be. "Besides, lives are fun. Friends and family have been interested in what I'm doing over here, and now that I have followers I don't recognize, they might show up, too."

"This is a thing?"

She raised an eyebrow. "That's kind of the point. It's how people get to know my work and how *Flights and Sights* discovered me in the first place, thanks to using the proper hashtag. Don't roll your eyes. And, yes, that's a thing. Anyway, thanks to them reposting my stuff, I've picked up a few more followers. Some even have their accounts set so they're notified when I do a live. So, yeah, it's a thing."

"But that doesn't mean I have to be a part of this," he pointed out. Really, he'd rather hang in the background—off screen.

"But you're a natural at it. Besides, do you know how many more people reacted to the stories with you in them? It's like double the engagement. My new followers are into you."

He harrumphed.

She only laughed. "Believe me, when you're just starting out, that's a big deal," she said. Her eyes sparkled when she smiled at him again, and that soft pang was back.

Damn, she was even more radiant than he'd ever noticed. He tamped down on the tide of lust that threatened to surface. Trouble was he damned near wanted it to. Was last night really going to be enough?

"Hey there, everyone!" She waved at the screen a few moments later and jabbed Blake in the ribs. "Jackson, hi! We're at the Lock Bridge in Cologne." She turned the camera so Blake could see himself on screen.

You two are still alive. You're not in jail. This is good.

He laughed at his best friend's assessment. "We're fine. Apparently, so are you."

He peered close enough to see the messages slowly appear and frowned. He still wasn't sure what all the fuss was about.

Her smile broadened. "Hi, Natasha. Yes, I remember you from Tina's bachelorette party, and yes, I promise what happened there stays there." She laughed, the sound rich and pure and completely unguarded. It shifted something inside him, lightened him, somehow, so that he couldn't help but grin. When could something as simple as hearing another person laugh make him feel so good?

"Getting around Germany is easy, when you have a guide, anyway." Zandra graced him with a smile. "I've yet to figure out the train system, but I can say that it runs very smoothly, and the trains always seem to be on time."

She winked at him. "Fortunately, I've had a great tour guide," she said, glancing at the screen again.

You two are so cute!

Are you two dating?

You look soooo happy!

He frowned as the words danced across the screen. "Ummm…"

"Nope." She pulled the phone back and laughed nervously. "Guys, no way. We are *not* dating. He's been a pain ever since I've known him—"

"Hey! I could say the same about you."

"You were worse."

Thunder boomed in the distance, and the sky opened up, a smattering of rain striking them as they raced for a small grove of trees at the park below.

"Oh my God, hold on guys," she said to the live. Laughing, they ducked underneath the closest tree, its branches protecting them like an oversize umbrella.

"This reminds me of that time in high school," she said, angling her phone until he appeared on the screen next to her. "I was at my brother's football game—remember that, Jackson?—and there was this guy on the team who was really hot." She laughed at the questions that scrolled up. "No, it wasn't Blake. He didn't play sports."

By the time he was in high school, he'd had a job. There was no time for sports. But she didn't remember that. "It was Sean Deveraux," he said. "You were pretty nuts over him."

"I'm surprised you knew." She turned those gorgeous baby blues on him.

Stay grounded, buddy. He swallowed and fought to stay focused.

"I never said a word to anyone. How did you know?"

"You didn't have to." How could he forget? Although why Sean had appealed to her was lost on Blake. She'd been too smart to truly want to be with the vacuous, narcissistic dude. Then again, it was high school, and they all had hormones to contend with.

He cleared his throat. "Whenever Sean showed up, your mood changed. It was obvious you had a thing for him."

While it had totally sucked, he'd reminded himself then, like now, that he had no business getting seriously tangled up with Zandra. It wasn't what she wanted, and he shouldn't want it, either. She was starting on a new career, a new adventure, while he was looking forward to having his boots in one place. He'd only hold her back.

She stared at him, curiosity written in the slight twist of her mouth. "Yeah, well, I remember the last football game of the season. The team was celebrating afterward, and I bribed my brother into letting me go along with them…"

She gazed at him, the corners of her mouth lifted in a smile so sweet Blake wanted to close the distance between them and feel her in his arms again, wanted to taste her one more time. He felt the answering grin on his face as she continued. "I knew rain was in the forecast."

"It was Seattle, after all," he reminded her. "You should've at least brought a raincoat."

"But I didn't want to ruin my outfit. And, of course, it rained. Do you remember what you did then?"

"No," he lied. He remembered it like it'd just happened, remembered the miniskirt and tight sweater that teased him the entire time he'd sat next to her, remembered the way he'd fought the urge to reach over and touch her. "Remind me."

"As soon as the rain started, you took off your jacket and held it over my head while we made a beeline for shelter." Her tone softened as her gaze held his. "Now that I think about it, that was a super-sweet gesture, Blake, and I never thanked you for it. It made me feel special." She blinked as if she'd just realized what she'd said. "I mean, mainly because you were a senior and I was just a freshman."

He swallowed. "Well, for the record, I didn't mind being soaked, and you bought me hot chocolate that night."

"I remember that part." Her voice softened. "Extra marshmallows."

"Extra marshmallows. You were right about those, by the way."

"That they made everything taste better?"

"It's the only way I'll drink them now. Same as you."

They grinned at each other as the rain drizzled around them, and once again Blake fought the urge to lean toward her for a kiss. One kiss. That's all he wanted.

Zandra blinked at the same time that the distant sound of an approaching train registered and slammed him back to reality. She turned back to her phone and the dozens of comments and heart emojis quickly scrolling along the screen.

You two are so cute together

You should totally be dating

Awww…that's so sweet!

I'm not liking this live…

The last one was from Jackson.

Yikes. Blake quickly tamped down any and all thoughts of sex with Zandra then set about trying to clear out the hopefulness that now flashed through him whenever she smiled in his direction. *Life plans, buddy. You've got life plans.* And so did Zandra. Their respective plans didn't include the other.

No matter how badly he suddenly wished they did.

Chapter Twenty-Four

Zandra took a deep breath and gripped the straps of her backpack tighter, determined to ignore Blake and the pull he'd had on her since they'd boarded the train for France this morning. Just this morning? How about since they'd spilled into bed the night before?

She smiled. At least she knew the sex wasn't a one-night fluke.

And now she stood surrounded by hearts, the glass pieces reflecting glints of light that filtered through the shop's windows in a kaleidoscope of colors.

Hearts. This was going to be an exceptional shoot.

"This place is gorgeous," she said to the young proprietors.

"Thank you." Jacques grinned at her. "We are very proud of our shop."

"Yes," Martine said, placing an arm around her husband's waist. "Jacques insisted that we open a shop here in Strasbourg, closer to where the tourists will find our work."

They were young, couldn't be past their twenties. Zandra looked around the shop again. "Do you create the glass yourself?"

"Some," Martine answered. "Some are from other local artists. But the hearts"—she pointed at a wall of various-sized glass—"the hearts are our creation. We specialize in them."

Zandra surveyed the wall, their vibrant hues encased in clear glass. "I love hearts. They're beautiful." She reached for one done in a smattering of purples, reds, blues, and yellows, the colors swirled together and encasing a key. "Why does this one have a key in it?"

"It's a symbol," Jacques explained. "The key is for the future. It takes the right 'key' to unlock it. To have it within the heart serves as a reminder that you must reach for the future with someone special to be truly successful, *non*? Otherwise, what is the point?"

"Yes," Martine said, looping an arm around her husband. "Aiming for what one wants in life is important, but to have it with someone special beside you while you do it? That's the ultimate achievement."

"That's so beautiful," Zandra breathed out.

"Why do you specialize in hearts?" Blake asked as he set up her computer on a glass case.

"It is tradition," Jacques simply said.

Martine moved a display aside to allow Blake access to a wall outlet. "We wanted to maintain the old way of blowing glass but also pay tribute to my grandparents."

"Let me tell it," Jacques said, beaming. "I want to practice my English."

"He's such a romantic." Martine graced him with a smile. "Go ahead."

He cleared his throat. "Grandpère et Grandmère, they blow the glass, many beautiful kinds, but they have a special place for the heart. All sizes, all colors. They say the heart is the sign of life. While it beats, there is time to love, to laugh, to live. But you must do so quickly because you do not know how long it will continue to beat."

Zandra slowly lowered the camera, her gaze immediately snaring Blake's. His stare was intense, almost daring her to come closer. Somehow nothing else registered but the stance he held a few feet away, the way his biceps flexed when he shrugged his jacket off, the way his mouth curled into a small smile.

She tightened her grip on the camera as something flowed between them, something she couldn't quite name, but powerful nonetheless. She swallowed. "That's a lovely story." Was that her voice? It sounded distant, like she might not have been the one to utter those words.

"Yes," Blake agreed, his gaze still holding hers. "I think so, too."

"And that is why we opened our shop here, so we can share their message," Martine added, breaking the spell and pulling Zandra back to the present. "Their life taught me that there is much value in tradition. Tradition does not need to always give way to the new. There is value in the old that lasts through many generations."

She arranged a pair of heart-stemmed champagne flutes. "So, we blow each piece in the traditional method where we can better control the finished product. Not like the machines used by some today."

"Machines have their place," Jacques pointed out.

Martine sighed. "He is still grumbling about the equipment he wishes to buy for a farmhouse we just purchased."

"There is much work to be done there," he groused. "The equipment will make it go fast."

"I like the idea of living on a lake or river, instead," Zandra offered. At least, it couldn't hurt to steer the conversation away from anything as contentious as a farmhouse that needed to be renovated.

"Now that's something I could appreciate," Blake said. "It needs to have lots of windows that overlook the water."

"Naturally. But the windows have to be the kind that open up so that on nice summer days I can hear the outdoor sounds. Especially if the kids are playing out on the deck."

"Chances are pretty good they'd be a handful, so there's no way they'd be allowed to be alone out there in the first place."

"Why not?"

"Too many opportunities for them to get in trouble. Water and kids don't mix."

Zandra rolled her eyes. "Okay, helicopter parent."

Martine made a tsking sound. "You two." She pointed a finger between Zandra and Blake. "You must iron out your differences before you get married. I promise it will make your lives go smoother."

Married? Zandra whipped her gaze toward Blake. "We're not—"

"—there's not a chance." He vehemently shook his head. "I've got things I need to do."

"That's right. And I've got plans, too. I'm just starting my photography career, and that's going to take a lot of travel and a lot of time. I couldn't possibly—" Married? She and Blake *married*?

"I'm going to law school as soon as my mom finishes medical school," Blake said.

"That's right," Zandra chimed in.

"Do you know how much time that's going to take?"

Zandra nodded her agreement. "It's a lot of time."

"Which means I'm going to stay put in one place—" Blake began.

"—while I travel all over the world for my photography job," she finished.

"And I'd never ask her to give up her dream."

"Not that I would."

"It wouldn't work." Blake crossed his arms.

"Nope, it wouldn't."

"It's impossible," they said in unison.

That's right. It was impossible. That was the most important takeaway from this experience. Anybody could see that.

"Interesting." Jacques tapped his fingers on a counter and grinned, his gaze darting between Zandra and Blake.

"Anything is possible," Martine added. "Look at me and Jacques. We were children, fighting over fire trucks and dolls, and then we became good friends, even when I went to university in London. Then one day, nature took its course until here we are now."

"Yeah, well, it's not that simple," Zandra insisted. Her heart might want one thing, but her brain knew better. She had her life to live, had to call the shots for it. Nowhere in the script was there anything about Blake.

"Oh, sure," Jacques said.

"I'm on my way to my dream career. It's all that matters." Her heart thumped in her chest, the words sounding a bit hollow, even to her ears.

Damn it.

Married?

Well, yeah, that was certainly in the plans, but down the road. Way down the road. There was a pretty good chance it wouldn't be Zandra, either.

But what if it was Zandra?

The thought circled through Blake's brain, taunting him in much the same way as her presence had since he'd started on this insane trip with her last week. Only, back then, he was pretty sure he could survive twelve days with no problems and certainly not the complications that could come out of it now.

Zandra took a deep breath, the movement causing her perfect breasts to rise, taunting him further.

He gave himself a mental shake. Thoughts like that weren't going to help him.

"I'm on Zandra version 2.0," she said. "Which basically means I don't have time for a relationship."

"Ah." Martine nodded. "You wish to improve yourself, and Blake does not help you do that."

Zandra turned toward him, her eyebrow arched. "It's not that. More like I don't need the distraction. And with someone like Blake, of all people? Not that you're a bad guy or anything," she quickly added.

"Good to know," he said drily.

"Let's face it. We're too different. Your time is owned by the Army for the next few years—"

"Until my mother finishes medical school."

"But then you're off to law school." She arched a brow. "And then you want to settle down," she said, blowing out a breath. "You probably want a family, too."

"Don't you?"

"I don't know." She frowned. "I'm not sure I want the responsibility of raising kids."

"For what it's worth, not all men expect a woman to take care of the kids on her own. I'd help raise them, too. It wouldn't be all up to my wife." He combed a hand through his hair. What was she trying to prove? That he had dreams, too? That he was willing to forge ahead to make them happen? That at this moment in time the thought of kids with Zandra didn't sound like a half-bad idea to him?

But it took two people spending actual time together to make it work. Like Tina and John, Martine and Jacques were proof of that. So no matter how good the thought, wanting to be with Zandra was nothing short of insane. "You make it sound like I'm out to crush someone's dreams just because I want to settle down and have a family one day," he said, crossing his arms in front of him.

"I'm simply pointing out how different *we* are."

"And there you have it," Martine said, clapping her hands together. "Passion. It is a necessary ingredient for two people, yes?" She turned to Jacques and fired off something in rapid French.

The younger man nodded sagely. "Yes, you are right." He pointed a finger from Zandra to Blake and back again. "These two, they will be together."

Blake shook his head and reached for a light. "We'd better get back to work."

Work he understood. Work was sane. This other stuff? Not so much.

Chapter Twenty-Five

Two days later, the whole glass shop exchange was still on Zandra's brain. She swatted the thoughts away every time they came up, but still...

She sighed, pulled on the straps to her backpack, and followed Blake along the dirt path toward the stables that housed the French farm's most prized agricultural possession: goats.

Goats weren't exactly her idea of fun, but then again, *Flights and Sights* had been re-posting her behind-the-scenes stories and had even put up their own Instagram story asking their followers to suggest something they'd wanted to see from Zandra. The overwhelming majority wanted goats. So instead of chilling and going through her photos today, they hit the road again.

Zandra put one foot in front of the other on the old dirt path. As long as she kept moving, she was fine, but after nearly twelve days of hauling stuff around like a packhorse, she was so over it. By a lot. But she'd also done some of her best work on this trip, so it was time to suck it up.

Besides, she was flying home tomorrow night and would be back in Seattle before long. If she was lucky, she'd be on to her next assignment in just a few weeks. Wasn't this what she wanted?

Oh, joy.

The knowledge should've brought her just that—joy. But there was a trace of something sharp, too, like a lance that'd been stuck into a corner of her heart, and she wasn't quite sure what to do about it.

"According to the guide, the stable's just around the corner, now. You sure you're okay to carry your pack?"

Blake's voice startled her out of her thoughts and another flash of awareness tripped through her when their gazes locked. How could she have known him through high school and most of her adult life yet not really seen him? Worse, how could she keep reacting to him like she was still *in* high school?

"I can take that for you if you like," he added. "You've got to be beat."

"Considering I've had little sleep in the past few nights? Yeah, I am a bit tired."

"Tired, huh?" A corner of his mouth lifted even as he took the backpack from her and threw it over one shoulder. How he managed to haul that on top of his own was beyond her. "And whose fault is that?"

Zandra's face bloomed all sorts of hot. "That's not fair. You snore."

"And that's what prompts you to wake me up in the middle of the night by straddling me?" he teased.

She fought her grin then gave up. "You got me there."

Blake stopped and faced her fully, his head tilted at an angle that made her want to lick that spot. "You know something?"

"Hmmm?" Really, if she did cave, how could he fault her, standing there and tempting her like that?

"You're beautiful."

Her breath caught. How could words so simple be so complicated and so amazingly delicious at the same time? "Thank you."

He reached a hand out and traced the curve of her face, the touch gentle, yet powerful enough to awaken a deep longing inside her. "Care to share what's on your mind, Zandra?"

"I'd rather show you." Her voice was breathless, flirty. Who knew a guy could bring it out in her? "When we're done with this and back in our hotel room, that is."

The corners of his mouth tipped up in a smile. "Let's find our contact, then, and get this photo shoot going."

Yeah, there was something about Blake that Zandra couldn't quite get out of her brain. He'd managed to invade her thoughts, not that it was hard, especially since they'd spent nearly every waking moment together since she'd landed in Frankfurt.

Frankfurt. Where it all started and where she'd leave from. Tomorrow.

Tomorrow. The day when this amazing trip ended, and Zandra 2.0 would be fully launched into the world.

Alone.

When she'd made reservations, she'd managed to snag the last seat, which meant she had to leave Blake behind. It hadn't mattered when she'd thought she'd be here with Jackson, but now...

The ache intensified, which was silly, really. It was probably better this way. Besides, she'd known from the beginning that there couldn't be anything between them, had told herself so, and had reminded herself often enough in the past few days. She stuffed the ache back and concentrated on setting up.

Fifteen minutes later, Zandra looked around the barn

and the dozens of white, bleating goats, some bearded, some with horns, some with neither. This should be interesting.

The lighting was adequate, and the subjects were clean—at least, they looked clean, even if they didn't quite smell that way. Trouble was, the only subject who interested her at the moment was the guy beside her, dressed in a pair of jeans and a gray T-shirt that stretched over broad shoulders and teased her with each move he made.

He turned and caught her gaze then winked as if he'd read her thoughts. Damn, the guy was hot.

"Come." Jean-Paul, their guide, motioned her outside with all the excitement of a six-year-old on his birthday. "We let the goats go now."

He pointed toward one end of the enclosed pen. "They decide where they wish to roam."

"You let them loose," she observed, one hand shading her eyes as she studied the fence.

He shrugged. "In many ways, they are like some humans—one cannot always tell them where to go." He grinned and indicated the farmland surrounding them. "If they choose, they may leave."

"Do they leave?"

"The males, sometimes. But they often return when they are ready to settle down, start a family." He rested his foot on the edge of the fence. "It depends."

Zandra raised an eyebrow. "Start a family? You're kidding, right?"

"Yes." His lined face stretched into an easy grin. "But there is one that is different." He pointed around the corner of the barn. "We separate the boys from the girls so that the milk is not contaminated, but there is one who breaks out of his pen all the time and will find his way to this one."

"Sounds like a guy," she said drily, raising the camera and checking the aperture settings. "Going to where the girls are."

"Oh, no. Not just any female, but one particular one. A doe we'd brought in last year. Lisette. From the beginning, he pays close attention to her and complains when we separate them."

She chuckled. "Sounds like boundary issues."

"Or more like love," Blake said.

Zandra lowered the camera and turned until she caught his neutral gaze. "You don't really believe that, do you?"

"Of course not," he scoffed. "I figured that's how most girls would see it."

Maybe, but there was a flash of something in his eyes, something she couldn't quite name. She could get lost in his eyes...

"Ummm..." Zandra separated her camera from the tripod. "Here, hold this, would you?"

He took it, his gaze not leaving hers, and she had the oddest sensation, like he was asking a question that she didn't know the answer to. She eased in a deep breath and turned, breaking the connection, breaking the bond that she probably only imagined anyway.

She had to put her head back in the game, stay focused on taking the best damned photos, photos that told a story. Even photos of goats.

"There's Billy now."

Zandra followed the direction of Jean-Paul's gaze where, sure enough, a goat trotted their direction. "Billy? You named the goat Billy?" She stared at Jean-Paul.

"Not me." The older man shook his head. "A little American girl who came to visit last year. She called him Billy, so we did, too."

"Billy goat," Blake snort-coughed. "Seems fitting."

"And here I thought you were making it up," she said, raising the camera toward the trotting goat then adjusting the camera's settings to accommodate the bright morning light.

Jean-Paul reached for his pocket as strains of a guitar

playing filled the air. "Excuse me," he said. "My wife."

"Go ahead." Zandra waved him off. "We'll be fine."

"Can't keep the goats apart," Blake said as the older man walked away, phone plastered to his ear. "Seems far-fetched to me."

"Then how do you explain Billy's presence?"

"Could be he's here for the chow."

The goat bleated a high-pitched, almost mournful sound as it approached the fence line, causing one of the goats that was feeding to stop and turn, its ears twitching as if listening for the call.

"Oh, yeah?" She nudged Blake. "Look at that. No one else is paying attention. Just her."

"I take it that's the object of his affection?" Blake asked. "She doesn't look any different from the others."

"Maybe not to you." Zandra walked along the fence line, toward the gate that led into the pen. Without her long-range lens, she needed to get closer to capture this story. And what a story it would be: love in all its glory prompts even a goat to defy all odds and find his way back to the one that's captured his heart.

It was sappy enough to work.

"Hey," Blake called. "Where do you think you're going?"

"To get a closer shot." She worked the latch on the gate, eyeing the two goats to ensure Lisette didn't plan a break of her own. "You know I don't have a long-range lens with me, and this is too adorable not to capture right."

He leaned against the fence and shook his head. "You're right about that. Go ahead."

"I wasn't asking permission, Blake."

When she lifted the latch, a hand came down firmly on hers. "Hey," he said. "I'm just trying to be supportive. That's all."

Her pulse quickened as she read the sincerity in his eyes.

This was a guy who'd stood by her the entire trip, helping to set up shots, getting her to the train station and on the right train. Hell, he even made her meals. In another time, another place, he'd be perfect.

The thought was intriguing and frightening at the same time.

She swallowed. "Thanks. I promise I'll be careful." The gate squeaked when she pushed it open.

"I'll be right here," he said.

She nodded and slowly walked toward the pair who nuzzled each other through a gap in the fence. Zandra kept her steps even, slow. Startling them could mean losing the perfect shot.

They looked so adorable together, like they truly belonged with each other and wouldn't let anything stand between them. Not even humans who thought they knew what was best for the pair.

Zandra could get behind that idea.

Looking through the camera lens, she snapped a couple of test shots, made adjustments to frame the goats, and crouched as she snapped frame after frame after frame. She moved as they did, finding angles that would best capture them—noses touching, mouths slightly open as they bleated. She crouched closer, still snapping away, her heart feeling for the two, and the cute rumbling noises they made as Lisette turned her face toward Zandra.

"That's it, girl," she murmured. "Good shot. Just like that. Keep facing me." A few more like this, maybe from the other side should—

"Zandra!"

The call registered a split second too late. Without warning, Lisette faced her head on, bared her teeth, made a running start, and attacked Zandra with all the force of a jealous female.

Chapter Twenty-Six

Holy shit.

Blake abandoned his backpack. He had no fucking idea if goats were prone to killing people, but he sure as fuck wasn't taking a chance.

Already on the ground, Zandra scrambled backward on all fours like a floundering crab. "Blake."

"Stay behind me," he said sharply, coming between her and the once docile Lisette. "No matter what move I make, stay behind me. Got that?"

"O-okay." No surprise her voice shook. Who'd have expected that a goat would fucking *attack*?

"I'm going to back us toward the gate. You ready?"

"Yeah."

He held the tripod legs, extending it like a weapon. Some weapon. He was pretty sure it wouldn't hold up against a charging goat, but Lisette didn't need to know that.

He waved his free arm, keeping his weapon pointed toward the goat, who seemed determined to get to Zandra. "Keep your distance, Lisette. I promise she doesn't want anything to do with your guy beyond taking pictures of the two of you."

What the fuck?

He was talking to a goddamned goat and holding a makeshift weapon. Good thing his Army buddies couldn't see him now.

Lisette flared her nostrils and made a sound akin to a honking horn. But then she backed up from him, and based on what he'd seen her do earlier, this wasn't necessarily a good thing.

They circled each other like a stand-off, and he heard Billy bleating behind him along with some serious fence rattling. Blake tensed. The goat was probably giving her attack strategies or something. Or maybe Billy figured his female was threatened so he'd tear the fence down. That wouldn't be good, either.

Movement caught his eye behind Lisette, toward the gate they'd entered from, but he didn't acknowledge it, focusing instead on the wide-eyed stare of the four-legged creature that seemed determined to take Zandra down.

Not on my watch.

It was bad enough the goat had gotten a good run at her. She appeared to be fine, but still…

Behind Lisette, Jean-Paul made a brisk movement, but there was no way Blake was taking his eyes off the jealous goat. Whatever the guy had planned, Blake was determined to keep the goat distracted.

The Frenchman uttered a few words, enough to make Lisette's ears turn in his direction. A goat that understood French? The idea was preposterous to Blake's logical brain, but at this point, it didn't matter. He just wanted to get Zandra out of here.

And while he wasn't quite sure how Jean-Paul managed it, the goat turned and trotted toward the fence where he and

Billy waited for her.

As far as experiences went, this ranked right up there as one of the most memorable. And the most ridiculous. Who the hell got attacked by a goat? Especially by a goat who seemed to be setting up some sort of a hookup with her goat boyfriend?

"You need to listen to me before you get hurt."

The words were uttered so casually, but irritation battled with panic and won. "I don't need to be protected."

Zandra clutched her camera close, adrenaline racing through her. She was shaken, no doubt about it, and she could've been seriously injured...but she wasn't. She was fine.

"Oh, yeah?" He crossed his arms and glared at her. "And what if I hadn't been here just now? What if Lisette hadn't let up?"

"She's not all that big. She just startled me, that's all."

"She knocked you down, didn't she?" Blake stalked toward her, all two hundred pounds of muscled control. "What did you expect me to do, Zandra? Stand around and watch her trample you? Maybe turn around and walk away while you *handled* things?"

There was an edge to his voice, a desperation that she couldn't quite put her finger on, but it was there nonetheless. He cared. Fiercely. She saw that in the way he protected his mother, her brother, her. The knowledge tore down the last defense she was sure was firmly nailed into place.

And that's when it struck her faster than a jealous female goat on the attack. Zandra had gone and done it. She'd barely won her freedom, won the ability to direct her life, and now she'd fallen for a man who had the power to distract her from what she wanted, from what she'd always wanted: to focus on her own needs and not worry about how her life would impact anyone else's. Especially Blake's.

Panic flowed through her, as heavy as the cheese fondue they'd had for dinner last night.

"I could've done this trip on my own, Blake. I didn't need you." Oh God. She was being unreasonable, and she knew it, yet she seemed powerless to take the words back. "I *don't* need you." She could do life on her own, *wanted* to do life on her own.

"You're not doing another video now, are you?"

"Better," she muttered, poking at the screen. "I'm taking the next train out."

"Hey." He gently turned her to face him. "What's going on? This isn't like you."

"Or maybe it is."

He raised an eyebrow but said nothing. And if she stared into his eyes for much longer, there was a better than good chance Zandra would change her mind, might actually come up with some compromise just to stay with him. She couldn't do that to herself.

"Look," she said, fighting to keep her tone even. "I need to focus on my own life. I can't worry about you or what you think, act, or feel. That's not my job." She stomped toward the open gate. She needed to get away from Blake, needed to put some distance between them.

She stared at her cell phone. There were numbers and letters and something that was supposed to be the train schedule. But what the hell was it even saying? She stopped beside the backpack she'd abandoned before entering the pen as a rush of dejection flowed through her, unearthing every shred of doubt she was sure she'd stomped out weeks ago. She tried to stuff them back, took deep breaths, and concentrated on the blue of the sky, the bleating of the goats, the chatter of farm workers who passed by.

What good was it? What good was any of it if she couldn't figure out something as common as a train schedule?

"Zandra? Are you all right?"

She waved Blake off. "I'm fine," she said, infusing every ounce of determination into her tone.

"You don't look fine." He scrubbed a hand over his face. "What's wrong now?"

The concern in his voice reached out to her, made her want to lean on him, lean into him. But that was the problem, wasn't it? She swallowed, took a deep breath, and stared into his eyes, and the caring she saw in them nearly undid her. "I can't do this."

"Do what?" He frowned. "I'm not following you."

She held out her phone. "This. Almost two weeks of taking the train and I can't even figure out the stupid schedule, let alone which section of the train we're supposed to be in or even where our seats are supposed to be on the damned thing."

God. If she couldn't figure out something that people all over the world did every single day, how the hell was she going to navigate life? Simple: she wasn't.

"I'm a complete failure." Maybe she was continuing to be unreasonable, but frustration spilled over almost as fast as the tears that trailed down her face. "I'm going to have to be an accountant the rest of my life."

And that was the worst of it. Everything she'd worked for, every battle she'd fought to get this far—the endless hours of walking the streets of Seattle, of taking shots of bakeries and homeless tent camps, of even the damned birds that dared scoop down on patrons at outdoor restaurants and food trucks. None of it meant anything in the end.

She'd failed.

"Hey. So you can't figure out a train schedule. So what? That doesn't mean you're failing at anything."

"Easy for you to say. You're not afraid of failing at anything. You've got it all handled, all under control. Everything from what you do for the Army to what you're going to do once you're out of the Army." She swiped at her tears. "Well, guess what, Blake? We're not all built like you. Not everyone is perfect."

"You're perfect to me."

The tears fell faster at the quietly spoken words. Maybe, but the fact remained *he* wasn't perfect for *her*. Not with where they were in their lives. It'd only be a matter of time before they were both miserable.

She raised her head and caught his gaze, caught the small smile that tinged his handsome face. "I mean it, Zandra." He swiped her tears away with his thumb and, hands on her shoulders, drew a deep breath, gazing at the cloudless sky like he was collecting his thoughts. "This time with you, it's been really special, because *you're* special."

"I am?"

"You are." He pulled her into a gentle hug, and all the reasons to walk away seemed to have escaped her. "I promise you are."

Their gazes locked, and there was that fuzzy feeling again, the one that made her think that just because they weren't *together*, together didn't mean they couldn't enjoy each other's company.

At least, that's what she told herself as she took a deep breath and held out her phone with the train schedule still on the screen. "Would you please show me one more time how to read this thing?"

Chapter Twenty-Seven

Blake took a deep breath and eased the tension out of his shoulders. He glanced at his companion as the train pulled into Stuttgart. "See? I told you you could figure out the train schedule." He squeezed her hand and smiled.

"I guess you were right." She flashed her megawatt grin at him, and his chest tightened.

He wasn't sure what the hell had happened back with the goats, had yet to figure out why she'd freaked, although it was likely from shock or something. She seemed better now. "You really are beautiful when you smile." The words flowed out of him smoothly, as naturally as if he'd uttered them forever.

"Thank you." She tilted her head to one side. "Your smile isn't so bad, either."

People rushed past them, and for the first time in forever, Blake didn't want to hurry, didn't want to rush to the next stop, the next destination. No. Instead, he wanted time to slow down, stand still, even. Because tonight was it. Their last night together.

His chest tightened even more. Probably indigestion

from the pizza they'd had before they'd boarded the train from France.

"Oh," she said as she bumped into him. "Sorry. I tripped."

"No worries. I'm tougher than I look." At least, physically he was.

He pointed toward King's Square and the crowd of people sitting on blankets and enjoying the late afternoon sunshine. "There's supposed to be some sort of concert tonight."

"You mean, like what's advertised on that huge billboard at the corner?"

"Oh, you can read. I forgot that."

She shrugged. "It's a tough skill, but I somehow mastered it."

Their shared laughter, her smile, the easygoing vibe they shared—this was the stuff he'd remember from their time together. This was what he'd have, and it'd be enough.

. . .

They slowly wandered through Stuttgart toward the hotel, and a sense of the inevitable swamped over Zandra. One night. One last night together.

She sucked in a deep breath then held it a moment before breathing out. After the incident at the goat farm, their unspoken truce was welcomed, the afternoon more enjoyable than she'd thought possible.

In less than twenty-four hours, she'd be on a flight to Seattle—without Blake.

He silently opened the door to their room and followed her in. Less than twenty-four hours and then they'd be back to…what, exactly? Could one go back to being acquaintances after what they'd shared?

She had to be reasonable about all this, had to know that what they'd shared might be special, but it certainly wasn't worth torpedoing her whole life for. She'd just won her freedom, for heaven's sake, and it sucked that she'd had to remind herself of that more and more these days.

The door shut behind them as she pushed her backpack off her shoulders. No matter what happened tomorrow, there was still what was left of tonight, and she was going to make the most of it. She turned to find Blake's gaze trained on her as he slid his backpack to the floor.

She ran her tongue over her bottom lip, but he kept his gaze firmly trained on hers. "Now what?"

"That depends," he said, stepping toward her.

"On?"

"Where this is going." He cocked his head to one side, a question in his eyes, one that she knew she should walk away from, but…

She kicked her shoes off. "I think we both know where this is going."

A small smile touched his mouth. "You're sure?"

"Absolutely." She'd reached him by then and dropped her gaze to his mouth. "Are *you* sure? Because I'd hate for you to have regrets later."

A corner of his mouth lifted. "A very wise woman once told me that life's too short to have regrets."

"Is that so? Well," she said, reaching a hand out and tracing her fingers over the front of his T-shirt with the outline of a skull printed on it. "She's right, you know. Life *is* too short to have regrets."

It was true. Which was why she'd take this time with Blake for what it was: laughter and tenderness and pleasure. She lifted her head and stared into his captivating eyes.

For the rest of her life, she'd remember his eyes, the way they revealed only what he wanted her to see. Like now. There was lust in there, all right, but this time it was mixed with something more powerful, something that played in concert with the hands that cupped her face, stroking softly, slowly, like he, too, was savoring the contact.

He lowered his head, nuzzled her nose briefly, then pulled back long enough to capture her gaze once more. "I'm going to make sure you won't regret anything tonight."

"Promises, promises." She gasped when he licked along her jawline, made his way to her neck, and when he reached it, she couldn't stop the stuttered breath she hadn't realized she was holding.

Her pulse quickened, the heat between them building in waves, each one more potent as he held her against him with one arm and lightly dragged a hand down to the valley between her breasts. "I've been thinking about these all day." He caressed the crest of one breast before moving to the other. "The way they move when you laugh or take a deep breath," he whispered against the pulse at her throat.

"Oh." She shuddered in another breath at his words, at the way he flicked his thumb over the sensitive tip of one breast, then the other, her senses tuned in to Blake. Only Blake and the delicious way he brought her body to life.

When he stopped and pulled back, her scrambled brain screamed a protest, her body at a loss for his heat, his touch. "Blake?" He didn't answer, and a moment later, her world turned on its axis, tilting her so she reached her arms around his neck for support.

"Yes?" He nipped leisurely kisses across her chin and carried her across the room, strolling past the old sofa and scuffed-up coffee table, past the TV stand that divided the sitting area from the bed like he had all the time in the world.

The bed shifted with his weight, and he laid her down, not breaking the kiss. The kiss. The mind-numbing way his mouth explored hers, tasting and teasing until she captured his tongue and gently sucked, heard his deep intake of breath. Good. Maybe now she stood a chance of giving as good as she got.

Still, Zandra concentrated on the feel of him on her, of the way his mouth explored hers, at the slight weight of his body as he pulled at the hem of her shirt and quickly stripped it off of her. Somewhere through the haze, her lack of clothing against his fully clothed body registered—just like the layers that hid him from her, layers she was determined to peel back, even if just for tonight.

She eased her fingers underneath the hem of his T-shirt and up his tight abs until she felt the thin mat of hair that covered his chest. He pulled back and groaned when she brushed a hand over his nipple. "What's the matter, Blake? Can't take as good as you give?"

His eyes burned her with that familiar lust, tempting her and issuing a warning at the same time. "Game on."

His mouth crushed down on hers, plunging her into a place where she had one foot in fantasy while a part of her fought to stay in reality, a place of pleasure versus a place of logic and reasoning. But who said logic and reasoning should have a place in this moment?

Zandra pulled back just long enough to pull Blake's shirt over his head, the skull printed on it replaced with the permanent one on his chest. She eased her fingers over it. "You never did tell me what it is about you and skulls."

"It's just a reminder that life's got an end date, so I need to live while I can."

She swallowed. "I believe that, too." That was exactly why, past tonight, she could afford no more distractions. She lifted her gaze to his and smiled. "I think we need to keep this party going."

Before long, the pile of clothes on the floor grew until all that she wore was a skimpy pair of panties.

"Better?" he asked with a lazy smile on his face.

She raised up onto one elbow and kissed the corner of

his mouth. "Getting there." She took his hand and led it to the small space between them and the scrap of black lace she wore. "I think you forgot a piece."

"Actually, I like to think of it as heightening the anticipation." He lowered his head and captured a thick nipple.

She moaned as want and need swirled into a mass so large it couldn't be ignored. "Blake." She uttered his name on a breathless sigh, desire surging through her in less time than she could process what was happening, how he owned her body, and how she wouldn't want it any other way.

And that's when Zandra knew the truth. Tonight, she was exactly where she belonged.

Chapter Twenty-Eight

Blake didn't want to rush things with Zandra. Not tonight. No, tonight he'd show her how much their time together meant to him, how much *she* meant to him, but damn, she was making it impossible to think straight.

She straddled him as he sat up, his back against the headboard, her face inches from his. "I want it hard and fast, Blake."

"What if I don't? What if I want to make you come more than a couple of times? What if I want you to hold out until you scream my name?"

A small smile touched her face, and she seemed undaunted by his words. "Then I guess we'll have to see how long *you* can last," she drawled, tracing a fingertip along his jawline.

Well, duh. That would be Zandra, all right. Sassy and stubborn and determined to do him in before the night was through.

"Do you want me to come too soon?"

"Of course not." She raised her hips to meet the thrust

of his hand. "It was just a small challenge. You know, to keep things interesting."

He raised an eyebrow. Small challenge? If he lived through this, he'd consider it a major victory.

Still, what was it about this woman that excited and maddened him at the same time? That made him crazy with want and need as well as drove him up the wall with her challenges? Whatever it was, he was in.

Blake raised his head and flicked a thumb over her exposed nipple then grinned at her sharp intake of breath. "Challenge accepted."

A tide of lust rolled through him, fast and furious and encouraging him to give in, to give her what she wanted. It'd be so easy, especially when she raised up and gently rubbed her wetness against his cock...

He closed his eyes. "Damn, that feels good," he ground out. He was pretty sure that he'd need more than sheer willpower to keep him from losing his fucking load too soon.

She bent forward, rubbed her gorgeous breasts across his chest. Somewhere along the way, she'd managed to remove her panties, the black lace against her creamy skin more inviting than any other piece of lingerie he'd ever seen on a woman.

Her eyes were hooded, her lips swollen from his kisses, and he'd never been more turned on than when she moved her hips against his erection, pulling a deep groan from him.

Blake gritted his teeth. Time for him to take charge. He moved quickly, flipping her onto her back before pinning her in place with one leg.

"Hey," Zandra protested. "I wasn't done playing yet."

"Oh, yes you are." Hell, he sure didn't know how much longer he would've lasted, not with the way she tortured him with slow, deliberate movements then speeding up again. His body didn't stand a fucking chance under these circumstances.

He scrambled to the edge of the bed, pulling her with him before kneeling on the floor. "My turn to play."

She reached for him at the same moment he spread her wide and touched his mouth to her. "But—ah…"

Her moans fueled him, made him alternate the pressure of his tongue on her clit before delicately sucking on it. And as soon as he did, she lifted her hips in a silent demand for more. He quickened the pace of his tongue, lapping and sucking, reveling in the tiny gasping sounds she made and the soft groans that confirmed he was doing things just right.

With one hand, he caressed her thigh, inching closer to her wet opening. She rose up onto her elbows and placed her heels on the edge of the bed, her eyes glazed as she watched him. Blake saw the desire build with each stroke of his tongue, each kiss against her clit. Her moans intensified when he stroked one finger down her slit then pushed inside her. He lifted his head and caught her gaze. "God, you're so wet."

"So come in me," she gasped. "You know you want to."

"Uh-uh. Not yet." He smiled. "You need to come first."

She bit down on her lower lip, her eyes glazing and hips lifting to meet the thrust of his hand. She lifted her chin up, and her eyes fluttered shut before she lowered herself onto the bed. "I'm…" she groaned, her body arching.

"That's it," he said, taking her clit in his mouth again.

"I'm—" She gasped, the word torn from her as she clutched the bed sheets.

He rolled his tongue against her clit then inserted another finger into her wetness, and the moment she tensed, he increased the pressure, increased the pace of his fingers, drawing her orgasm out as long as possible.

"That was unbelievable."

He smiled, masculine pride rushing through him. "We're just getting started."

Zandra slowly floated back down to Earth, the world crystallizing in front of her as the throes of her orgasm faded and Blake's face, just a few inches away, came back into focus.

She smiled. "We're just getting started, huh?"

He shifted then stilled like he was studying her.

"What do you see?" she asked.

He smiled and shook his head. "You're just so beautiful. Not just the exterior, but here, too," he said, holding a hand over her heart. "Inside. Where it matters."

She tried to make light of it, *wanted* to make light of it, but the sincerity in his voice, in his touch, in his look... there was no way she could. "Thank you," she said, her heart bursting with an unnameable something.

Without another word, he leaned down and kissed her, lightly skimmed his mouth over the sensitive spot behind her right ear.

"Oh my God," she groaned as soon as he licked it. "That makes me insane."

He licked again, bolts of energy zipping through her like electrical wiring gone haywire. She groaned, her body restless once more.

"Why do you think I do it?" he whispered, nuzzling her ear before tracing the shell back down.

She lifted her hips so that his stiff cock was perfectly nestled at the juncture between her legs. There. That was better. So. Much. Better.

Her eyes drifted shut, and she shifted, allowing his cock to glide over her clit once. Twice. The sensations were heightened by the feel of his mouth against her neck.

She widened her legs, but he pulled back. "No," he said. "I'll rub my cock against you all you want, but that's it."

"Wait. That's it?" She offered her best pout. "Don't you

want to be inside me?" She lifted her hips again.

This time, he groaned. "More than you know. But not yet."

He lowered himself until he was nestled against her again, but she saw the way he gritted his teeth, knew that this was costing him. The knowledge touched a part of her, made her aware of all the layers that made Blake who he was: fiercely loyal, tender, and giving among them.

She shut her eyes and lifted her hips once more, lightly grazing herself against his stiff cock, but it was more than enough in her hypersensitive state. She bit down on her lower lip then nearly jumped as he increased pressure against her clit.

"Oh." She blew out a sharp breath as he did it again, and again, each time rocking against her a little longer, a little harder, his movements a whole lot sexier.

She couldn't contain the swell of emotion gathering force, pulling her forward, demanding she give in. She rubbed against him harder, holding onto his back and arching up so that she rubbed against him just right.

The pressure built, release just one stroke, one light stroke away.

And when it came, the tide was fierce, sweeping her up and over and… "*Blake.*"

He continued to rock against her, murmuring praise and raining kisses on her mouth, her chin, her cheek, and then he was gone.

When he returned a moment later, he tore open a condom packet and sheathed himself.

She angled her hips, an invitation she was pretty sure he'd accept this time.

"You're so wet," he groaned as he sank deep inside her, setting the pace with each slow plunge.

Zandra held his gaze and thrust upward, her legs wrapped

around him. "So good," she moaned as her eyes slowly shut.

The feel of him inside her was powerful, each stroke gliding her closer to the edge, closer to another release.

"Baby, I'm close…"

Zandra arched, her body clenched as she went over the edge, with Blake not that far behind her.

"Well," she whispered a short while later. With a smile, she reached up one hand and traced his chin, the stubble on his face rough against her forefinger. "That was amazing."

It was more than amazing, actually. It was powerful, like lust mixed with a healthy dose of something that she couldn't quite put her finger on.

He grinned and kissed her nose. "Don't move."

"Like I can get my legs to work after that."

He chuckled as he moved off of her then pulled the covers up to her chin. A moment later, he returned and pulled the covers back.

She blinked her eyes open. "A warm towel." She rose onto one elbow and watched as he carefully bathed her thighs.

Blake. Dear, sweet, amazing Blake. It felt like she'd searched a dozen lifetimes to find that one opportunity, that one chance to frame the perfect shot with a special man, only in the end, the timing was off.

When it came right down to it, there was more than one "perfect" man, more than one person with whom she'd find that spark. Right now she needed to focus, no matter how tempting Blake was. She had to think about herself.

Despite all the logical reasons to maintain an emotional distance, her heart ached with the kind of force only reserved for romance novels or sappy ballads. This wasn't good. Not good at all.

"You okay?" he asked, lines of concern on his face as he tossed the towel aside.

Tears moistened Zandra's eyes, and she quickly looked

away. "Yes, of course."

"Good." He snuggled next to her and pulled her close. "You're pretty amazing, Zandra."

"I like when you say my name."

"It's a unique name, that's for sure. Then again, you're pretty unique." He kissed the top of her head, the movement so sweetly endearing her heart ached.

She closed her eyes and savored the moment. This was it, their last night together. Tomorrow she'd be on a plane back to Seattle—without him.

She alone was responsible for the course of her life, she alone chose the direction it went, and who, if anyone, would come on that journey with her. She needed to fly fast, which meant flying alone.

Opening her eyes, she fought back the lump in her throat and tried like hell to concentrate on this moment. Blake's gentle touch, his smile...the way he made her feel...*especially* the way he made her feel.

She had so much she wanted to do with her life, starting with her photography career. She wanted it, and she'd earned a start in it. So how come her heart felt like it was shattering into a gazillion ragged pieces?

Because it was.

She laid on her side, one leg thrown over Blake's, and let the pain wash over her. There was no shame in feeling. It's what had allowed her to take the photos the e-zine editor loved so much that she was offered a chance at a full-time position with *Flights and Sights.* She owed it to herself, to the world, to pursue her passion.

And this short interlude with Blake left her with a lot to smile about, didn't it? Like the skull inked onto his chest, it reminded her of the brevity of life and the need to seize each moment.

Zandra traced her fingers over the short hairs on his chest

and tried to commit every hard ridge to memory. It would be all she'd have left after tonight.

"Blake?"

"Hmmm?"

"Do you believe in fate?"

"I believe you make your own fate."

"So do I." She cleared her throat. Damn, this was going to hurt, but there was no way around it. "Please don't come to the airport with me tomorrow."

The hand that had absently traced her hip came to a stop so briefly, she thought she'd imagined it. "Okay."

He hadn't argued, hadn't demanded she rethink her stance, hadn't fought for her, for them.

Because there was no them.

And she needed to accept that.

Chapter Twenty-Nine

Blake felt like shit. Not the I-drank-too-fucking-much kind of shit, but more like the someone's-run-over-me-with-an-emotional-tank kind. And there was only one way he knew of to get rid of it. Which was why he was pushing himself so hard this morning.

His heart pounded with each stomp of his running shoes on the sidewalks around Stuttgart, past the Tesla store, and toward the construction site that seemed to buzz with the same kind of activity that stuttered through him.

Blake needed to forget, needed to remember, needed to figure out which way his head had to be screwed on so he didn't screw up his life—or Zandra's, for that matter.

Please don't come to the airport with me...

Even now the words stung, her quietly spoken request reverberating through him as he continued to pound his way back to the hotel. Cars honked, buses honked, every fucking vehicle on the roadway seemed to fucking honk.

He forced his focus on the next step, the next footfall, the next breath he took in instead of the heaviness in his heart. It felt crushed, almost, like the weight of the world had stomped it into less than half its original size.

Please don't come to the airport with me...

How could Zandra do it? How could she walk away from what they had like it had meant nothing to her?

Sure, she had goals, had plans for herself. So did he, for that matter. The last thing Blake wanted to do was stomp out her dreams. She'd fought too hard for her freedom. He saw that, saw the respect she'd earned from others with the photos she took. She had talent in spades, and she needed to explore it. She needed to grow herself.

As for him? Well, he had obligations, duties, responsibilities. He had a fucking Life Plan, for God's sake, one he wasn't going to deviate from no matter what—or who—walked into his life.

Except he'd do it for Zandra.

That's what freaked him out.

He waited for a break in traffic before crossing the heavily traveled street.

The fact he cared about her couldn't be denied.

But did she care about him?

Please don't come to the airport with me...

Sure, she'd made that ridiculous request, but what if she hadn't really meant it? And what if he presented terms that were mutually agreeable to both of them? Things between them were good, better than good, really, so why should things change once they left Germany? At least, until he figured out where his next assignment would take him.

But given his position on the Special Forces team, he had a luxury afforded to so few in the Army—he could choose his next post. And right now there were two generals vying for his attention.

That's what he'd do. He'd take the post closest to Seattle that trained Special Forces soldiers, which meant moving to

North Carolina. Sure, it still meant they were on opposite sides of the country, but he could take long weekends every now and then, and maybe she'd get an assignment close enough so they could see each other.

Zandra was obviously unwilling to let go of her freedom, so he'd work with it. If he did that, maybe he could convince her to take their relationship to the next level.

As he neared their extended stay hotel, Blake's heartbeat increased, and he was sure it was more than just the exercise. He raced up the stairs, careful not to knock over the potted plant at the landing.

Outside their room, he took a deep breath and gathered his thoughts. They would be logical, orderly, and ones that she'd agree to. Because why wouldn't she? They could enjoy each other's company and still go after what they wanted in life, right?

Blake contained his excitement and pushed open the door. Her flight didn't leave until tonight, and even though she was flying out of Frankfurt, it was a few hours until she needed to catch the train.

As soon as the door opened, he stopped.

The lights were off, but the blinds were wide open...and Zandra was gone.

• • •

Zandra stood off to the side in Frankfurt's train station terminal and watched the crowd go by. She'd done it. She'd figured out the schedule, gotten herself to the station in Stuttgart, and even caught the right train to Frankfurt. Blake would be so proud. Too bad she couldn't tell him.

Even worse, the victory now rang hollow.

Her heart hurt, but she'd accept it, and it would heal in time. Because what else could she do? Even now, she had proposals in place with three other e-zines, so it wouldn't be long before she'd head off to a new assignment, even if *Flights and Sights* didn't take her on for something new right away.

And Blake? Well, he needed to find a woman who could be with him, no matter the direction his dreams took him. She couldn't give him that.

The pain intensified, and she eased in a deep breath, cinched her backpack tight around her waist, and dragged her roller bag in one hand and her suitcase in the other.

Situational awareness...watch the crowd...make sure to keep your possessions close.

She shouldn't be surprised that Blake's instructions echoed in her head. They made sense, after all, and helped make her a better world traveler, which was exactly the trajectory her career would take her. And exactly what she wanted to do with her life, right?

Right.

She studied the signs, following the ones that led to the adjoining airport. Yeah, she was being a coward, but after last night, after the way Blake took care of her and held her until she fell asleep, there was no way she was hanging around this morning. Nope.

She'd done the right thing, quickly packing her stuff and heading out a few minutes after he'd left on this morning's run. It might be a coward's way of handling things, but it already hurt like a mother, and she wasn't going to make it worse by hanging around and saying good-bye.

Besides, she hadn't been entirely sure she'd be able to figure out the train schedule and allotted enough time in case she ended up headed somewhere funky—like Belgium. God knew that had been entirely possible.

She hoisted her bags onto the escalator that led to the airport terminal entrance, careful not to sideswipe the swarm of nuns that had joined her on the moving walkway.

Really, it was a good thing she was doing this travel thing on her own. Sure, Jackson would follow her around and be her assistant whenever he got the chance—that's what big brothers were for. But in those instances when she had to do stuff on her own, knowing how to navigate the world was a big plus.

She just wished she had the help of one hot-looking, well-traveled, Army Captain.

Chapter Thirty

"What's up with you?"

Blake looked up from the stack of papers he'd had his nose buried in for most of the morning. "Good morning to you, too, asshat," he replied as Jackson entered the office Blake had temporarily commandeered and plopped onto one of two uncomfortable chairs parked in front of Blake's desk. "You're back."

"If you'd open your text messages, you'd see that I came home three days ago." Jackson slouched against the chair back, a sure sign there was some serious shit going down.

"Can't be anything with Uncle Sammy or I'd have gotten something official, too." He carefully capped the pen he held, almost sure he knew why his best bud was in his borrowed office at six a.m. on a Saturday morning, out of uniform.

Jackson cocked his head to one side. "You too good for me now?"

"Why the hell would you think that?"

"You're avoiding me."

Not exactly. More like Blake was avoiding Zandra.

Anything that Jackson was doing socially, outside a guys' night, meant that there was a good chance his sister would be close by. And while it'd been a week since Europe, Blake wasn't in any mood to see Zandra again. Not so soon, anyway.

"Since you're likely to PCS out of the states, I thought you'd be doing something other than burying yourself in paperwork."

A permanent change of station was exactly what he needed, and the move couldn't come soon enough. He raked a hand through his hair. That's what he *wanted*. It was a chance to up the training for a new batch of Special Forces soldiers, a chance to teach them skills to keep them safe, a chance to make a difference in this crazy world.

"You making an offer?"

"How about something fun like camping out by a lake or hiking Mt. Rainier?"

Hanging at a lake sounded like a good idea. Preferably one with the Swiss Alps surrounding it and a gorgeous woman sitting next to him, feeding the swans.

Not helpful, buddy.

"Can't. Don't have the time."

"Well, you coming to Anthony's tonight? To celebrate Zandra's promotion at *Flights and Sights*? She's pretty stoked."

He stopped and blankly stared at the paperwork in front of him. She'd worked so hard, and he was so damned proud of her. But the last place he wanted to be was somewhere he wasn't wanted. "Can't. Got too much going on."

And that's what he'd been doing since getting back— burying his nose in paperwork, taking care of business, exactly the way he was supposed to.

Too bad things weren't the same. He used to get off on doing things better, faster, turning out quality soldiers ready for field experience. Now...well, things were just different.

Not that he didn't care about all that. He did. Life just wasn't the same since he'd come back from Germany, which was insane. He was tracking forward, toward law school and the career he'd always wanted.

But a big part of him felt like it'd been left in that Stuttgart hotel room.

Blake squared his shoulders and sucked in a deep breath. He was taking care of his responsibilities to his mother, to his sister, and to himself. Nothing wrong with that. Nothing at all.

Not long ago, he'd have sworn it was all he'd ever wanted. Now he wasn't so sure…

"Do you even know where you want to head to next?" his best friend interrupted, snapping Blake back to the present.

He tapped his fingers on the worn wood desk. "No. Maybe."

"That's decisive." No missing the sarcasm in his best bud's voice.

"Japan's a possibility." Blake shrugged. "New training team, best equipment, easy access to home. You know, in case Mom needs me."

With the added benefit of the Pacific Ocean separating him from Zandra.

Blake stared across the desk at his best bud. "You know, the more I think about it, Japan's looking pretty good."

That was logical. And right now, to get where he wanted, logic had to trump everything else.

· · ·

Zandra glanced around the restaurant at the close-knit group of people who'd loved and supported her for as long as she remembered. "Thanks for coming by, everyone." She grinned and waved, exchanging hugs and pleasantries.

"We knew you could do it, Zandra!"

"You're definitely on your way!"

"When's the e-zine issue coming out? I need to subscribe."

This was it. All her hard work coming to fruition. This was what she'd wanted, what she'd dreamed of, for years. Through every accounting class and summer bookkeeping jobs through college, through the realization that none of it appealed to her, through the knowledge that these people loved and supported her decision to become a full-time photographer.

"Tell everyone about your next assignment." She glanced up and caught her father's proud smile.

"You earned it, sweetheart," her mother added.

That her parents had turned out to be more supportive than before was an added bonus.

Zandra sucked in a deep breath, still proud, but the giddy feeling not half as strong as she'd once thought it would be. "They're flying me to Guam."

"Guam? Where is that? Sounds exotic," someone asked.

"It's in the South Pacific." Truthfully, she'd had to Google the location of the easternmost U.S. territory, barely a dot on a world map. There was a lot of ocean between Seattle and the tiny island.

She sipped her beer. Cold. Not warm like the Germans drank it.

Well, with any luck, she'd end up on assignment in that part of the world again one day. She looked around the table at the crowd of family and friends who chatted, ate, drank, and celebrated with her. For the moment, she'd bask in her next assignment.

"I saw Blake today," Jackson said beside her.

At her brother's words, Zandra froze, blinked, then slowly lowered her bottle. "Oh?" She forced a smile. "He's still in Seattle?"

They hadn't talked about his next duty station or when he'd leave, and now she couldn't stop the curiosity insanely tracing through her.

"Yeah." Jackson frowned. "I told him he should be here tonight. You know, since he played tour guide and all."

"Yeah?" Her heart hammered, and she had to force herself not to look toward the front of the bar, forced herself not to look for Blake.

"Yeah. He said he was too busy." Jackson eyed her as he took another swig of beer then swallowed. "It makes me wonder what the hell happened in Europe, but it's warring with a part of me that swears I don't really want to know. Watching you two in that live was bad enough."

She straightened in her seat and stared him down. What happened with her and Blake was none of her brother's business. "You should listen to that part of you."

Jackson narrowed his gaze and opened his mouth like he wanted to say something then changed his mind. He nodded a moment later.

Europe was a done deal, wasn't it? She needed to quit looking back because that's not where her future lived.

She took a deep breath and smiled, forced herself into the present and the band of people who'd shown up to celebrate with her. "This next assignment is a bonus, of sorts, even though I'm still new." Right along with the nice financial one she'd been given. The real bonus was when her editor had made it clear that Zandra was destined for exciting assignments.

She frowned even as she quelled the sharp longing in her chest. She was getting everything she wanted, and it somehow wasn't half as great as she'd once expected.

Because she couldn't share any of it with Blake.

Chapter Thirty-One

All things considered, life in Japan was pretty good.

Blake was training a new batch of soldiers, the weather was pretty decent, and in the three weeks since he'd arrived at the military base in Okinawa, he'd made two trips into Tokyo, once to scope out the temples he'd finally gotten his mother to admit she'd wanted to see, and now to meet up with her while she was on summer break.

Despite his suggestion, Constance Monroe had insisted she hadn't needed to drop her backpack off at the Airbnb before hitting the sights. Then again, getting his mother to change her mind about anything often took a great deal of time and patience, both of which had seemed to be in short supply these days.

"Are you sure you're okay?" His mother laid a gentle hand on his, the touch soothing much as it had when he was a little boy and she worked two jobs and still managed to be patient with him.

He looked up from his tea cup and traced a thumb over the delicate etching on its side. "Yeah, why?"

His mother's shrewd eyes narrowed slightly. "You haven't said much since I got here."

"Sorry." He dragged in a deep breath and regarded the woman to whom he owed all that he was. "Just a bit tired."

"Seems to me I'm the one who should be tired after crossing a few time zones and sitting for more than ten hours." She straightened in her seat when he didn't offer a response. "Don't get me wrong, Blake, because I'm glad to be here, but you're the one who insisted on this trip."

"I thought you'd said you'd always wanted to visit the Tokyo temples."

"Not all thirteen thousand of them," she said drily. "And certainly not all in one day." She raised her teacup and sipped. "I would've been just as happy chilling—as you kids call it—after my exams last week."

Of course she would have. She never complained and didn't ask for much. It's one of the many reasons her being here was so important to him. "You've worked hard, Mom. You've earned this time to visit temples or do whatever you want."

"At the risk of sounding ungrateful, what I wanted most after that brutal quarter was to sleep."

"Sleep?" He raised an eyebrow. "You can't be serious."

She lifted a corner of her mouth in a crooked smile. "Sleep. Not that I'm going to get much of it once I start my hospital residency, but I figured I should grab some while I can."

"Why didn't you tell me?"

"What? That I'm perfectly capable of taking care of myself? That I'd make it to Japan one day? That I got through chemistry and physiology without your help, so I could most certainly find my way around Japan—or any country—just fine without you?" She tilted her head. "Would you have believed me?"

He raised an eyebrow. Would he have believed her? He'd
vowed as a kid to do everything he could to protect his mom,
to help her achieve her own dreams since she'd sacrificed so
much to give him and his sister a shot at life. He'd been willing
to do the same for Zandra. "Yes, I know you're capable of
taking care of yourself, Mom."

She gave him a small smile then relaxed against the
wooden chair. "You have something on your mind." His
mother stared. "Tell me about it."

He tapped his fingers on the table and stared out the
window. Maybe his mother was right. The more he thought
about it, Zandra didn't learn the train system until he'd had
to practically duct tape his mouth and not tell her what to
do when they'd left the goat farm for Stuttgart. If he hadn't
interfered all the other times, she'd probably have caught on
much more quickly.

"I've been a total ass," he muttered, slumping forward.
"A complete and total ass."

"Now I think you're being a bit dramatic, Blake."

He shook his head. "You don't understand. I took that
away from her."

"Who?" The gently asked question made him sit up. He
searched his mother's eyes.

"Zandra," he finally said, watching her closely.

True to form, she didn't pry, didn't ask complicated
questions, but simply said, "Go on. Tell me what's been
happening."

Some guys would never swallow their pride or bare their
souls to anyone, let alone a parent, but his mother had never
let him down. Ever. He trusted her to have his back as much
as he trusted his battle buddies.

"It all started when I met Zandra in Germany. Back
when she'd gotten her first assignment for that e-zine." Blake
let it all out, from the way he'd admired Zandra's work ethic,

her insistence on perfection from each shot she took, to the hours she spent editing the photos she'd taken, to even the time she'd spent posting things on social media.

He told his mother all of it, right down to Zandra's resilience when someone had stolen her camera lens, to the way she'd tried and tried and tried to figure out the train schedule until she'd finally nailed it on her last day in Germany.

"So what happened that's got you all upset?" she quietly asked when he'd finished.

He looked up from the tea that had grown cold long ago. "Nothing. She just... It's just..." What the hell was he even trying to say? That Zandra tended to tie him up in knots? That the time they'd spent together was more special than he'd thought possible? That the thought of not seeing her smile again, touching her, laughing with her ate at him so hard that he was having trouble sleeping?

If he were really fucking honest with himself, it was the realization that he'd willingly give up what he wanted for his life for someone who was his polar opposite.

He spiked a hand through his hair and sucked in a deep breath. He was thoroughly fucked.

"She's special," his mother finally supplied. "Am I right?"

He glanced up. "She is. And that's where I fu—umm, screwed up." He ducked his head and tapped his fingers on the wood table top. "She'd taken some amazing photos, stuff I don't think I'd ever seen before. I mean, it's like she'd touched the soul of whatever she was shooting, whether it was people dancing or a piece of chocolate."

"I understand she's really talented."

"She is." He continued drumming his fingers on the table. "But afterward, when we were back in Seattle, I found out about the recognition she'd earned from *Flights and Sights*, that they'd given her a bigger assignment, and I didn't support her. I didn't acknowledge her success, I didn't even send her a text. I..." He looked away. Confessing this to his mother was beyond embarrassing and something he had to do. "I ignored her."

"Why? That's not like you."

"Because I'm scared, Mom, scared of what'd happen if I turned my focus from what *I* want to do with my time and bent to someone else's wants." He sucked in another deep breath and tried like hell to stay grounded. "I mean, think about it. First chance I get, I'm headed to law school, which means staying put. Meanwhile, Zandra's just starting her career, one that she'd been dreaming of for years. She wants to travel, to take pictures all over the world. How could I ask her to give that up? Ever?"

"Law school?" She sat up, a frown on her face. "You want to go to law school? How did I not know this?"

"Ummm...well..." He scrubbed a hand over his face. Now he'd gone and done it. He hadn't planned on sharing anything with his mother until after her graduation day.

"Blake, tell me the truth. How long have you wanted to go to law school?"

He glanced up and caught the no-nonsense look on her face. No way could he lie to her now. "Since I was a kid."

"Then why in the world did you insist on helping fund *my* college plans? You and your sister both swore you wanted military careers. Why didn't you go after your dreams first? Because I'm assuming Lily doesn't want to stay in the Army, either."

"You'll have to ask her." He made a mental note to text his sister. She was probably still doing drills in Australia and wouldn't get his message anytime soon. "Look, you're our mom, and you gave up a lot for us." He swallowed deeply but forced his voice to remain even. "You'd just started college when Dad died. You gave all that up and made sure there was a roof over our heads and food on the table. You helped put us through college, too. Now it's your turn. You deserve a shot at making your dreams come true."

"And you don't?" Her shoulders slumped as her eyes searched his, and he had the uneasy feeling this convo wasn't ending anytime soon. "Oh, Blake, ever since you were young, you've been taking care of everyone else instead of doing what you wanted. My God, you even learned how to cook so that you were better than I was by the time you were fourteen."

What did she expect him to do? Let her do it all on her own? "You were busy, you held down two jobs, so I helped where I could." He shrugged. "Besides, it was either that or starve." He grinned, hoping the conversation could be diverted to safer topics. "So which Japanese temple would you like to see next?"

"You took care of your sister," she said, clearly ignoring his attempt to steer the conversation. "You held a job when you were in high school, you didn't play sports like the other kids, and through it all, you never complained."

"I learned that from you." He flashed her another grin. "So how about that next temple, huh?"

"And you're still doing it."

Damn it. He blew out a breath. Clearly, his mother was determined to finish this conversation. "You mean not complaining? Because I could start now."

She shot him a hard stare. "You're still playing the caretaker role for people instead of doing what you want to do with your time. Case in point: your trip to Germany."

"I did it because it was the right thing to do," he protested. "Zandra had never traveled overseas before."

"Maybe so, but did you even think twice about the concert tickets to one of your favorite rock bands that you'd had to give up?" She eyed him. "And now I find out that not only do you want to go to law school, but instead of getting out of the Army and doing it, you re-enlisted so you could pay for me to go to medical school."

He blinked. Jeez. He'd forgotten about the concert tickets, hadn't thought twice about them since he'd given the pair to a homeless vet program to be raffled off. "First off, it was just a concert. Secondly, like I'd said, I'll get my chance after you graduate."

"Which I now realize conveniently falls around the time your Army contract ends," she said drily. She blew out a breath and stared at him. "But you do know this overprotective mode you're in is probably part of the reason you're having trouble with Zandra."

Well, that'd teach him to want to change topics again. "I already said I wouldn't ask her to give up photography."

"Who says you have to ask her to give anything up?"

Blake stared. "Well, I'm not giving up *my* plans."

"Who says she'd ask you to do that?"

Maybe she wouldn't, but he knew that successful relationships meant investing time in each other. How could they do that if hundreds of miles of air space separated them? Maybe an entire ocean or continent, too? He was dumb enough at one point to think it could work, but he knew better now.

"Honey," she said, her voice gentle, "that's not what's at the root of all this. The question you have to ask yourself is whether or not your overprotective behavior is going to change anything."

"What are you getting at?" He frowned. "Maybe I do take care of the people I care about, but I don't expect anything back from them, nor do I expect it to change anything in my life."

"Not even bring your father back?"

He stilled at the quietly asked question then swallowed. He and his mother had never talked about that night, and while he'd expected the topic to come up one day, he hadn't thought it'd be in a tiny tea house in the heart of Tokyo. Yet somehow, every reason to hold back seemed to fall away as easily as the sun breaking through the clouds over the city. "I couldn't help him, you know."

"You were only four. Surely you're not blaming yourself for his death, are you?"

A sharp pain struck him in the chest, and he breathed deeply, tried to ease it. "I could see them," he said quietly, his mind's eye taking him back to that fateful night when his life was forever changed. "Those two guys in the convenience store. I was in my booster seat, and I could see Dad trying to protect the gas station attendant. Then the gun went off."

He'd alternated between screams and cries until his mother held him an hour or so later. He remembered regularly putting his toys away after that in an effort to stop his mother's tears, and although they eventually stopped falling, he'd learned to keep his room clean and did laundry as soon as he could move a stepladder close enough to the washer, and also learned how to cook...

Holy shit. He blinked. That's really when it had all started for him. He stared across the small table as scene after scene continued to play from some deep recess in his brain. "You're right," he finally said. "I've been doing it practically my whole life and never realized it."

She leaned forward. "Blake, when your father died, I was almost sure my life was over. But then I realized something."

"That you had kids who needed you, so that's when you rallied."

"No." She shook her head. "I realized I had *myself* to live for."

He raised an eyebrow. Not the answer he expected, especially since his mother had been pretty selfless, sacrificing much to give him and Lily the best she could. That his grandfather had been around for a few years was a bonus.

"Make no mistake, I loved your father. To this day, he was the most amazing man I've ever met, a man I respected and cherished and who I knew felt the same way about me. But I also know that I decide the course of my existence, no matter who is a part of it. Now you have to do the same." She smiled encouragingly. "Because no matter how protective you are of the people around you, your dad's not coming back."

He blinked at the deep stab of emotion in his chest, unable to deny it any longer. That he'd spent most of his adult life trying to bring him back was a huge bitch slap right now. "You're right," he said through the lump in his throat. He was powerless to change things, but he could affect the future—his future.

And maybe Zandra's, too?

"Your life isn't in the past," his mother continued. "That's where you've been living, but it isn't really *living*. Living is now. Living is doing what's right for you, for what you want, not just what other people want, because your life matters, too. You know, some would argue that my life didn't work out. I would argue otherwise. I raised two kids then took a chance on reaching for my dreams thanks to those kids. It took a long time, but look at me now."

She sat back and toyed with her teacup. "If you're brave enough to see where things go with Zandra, no matter what happens, I think you'll discover that your life will work out, maybe even better than you expected."

He blew out a breath and stared out the window at the throng of people. Maybe his mom was right. She usually was. Maybe choosing to be with Zandra didn't have to mean giving up his own dreams. Maybe there was a way they could make a long-distance relationship work.

He reached into the front pocket of his jeans and felt the unmistakable glass heart. At first, he was sure it was the dumbest impulse buy he'd ever made, but now hope bloomed like the last of the cherry blossoms on the tree across the street.

All he had to do was figure out a way to convince Zandra to take a chance on *them*.

Chapter Thirty-Two

It had been three days since Zandra had landed in Guam.
Unlike the fast-paced European trip a few weeks ago, life on
the tropical island was far more relaxed, as were the native
Chamorro people. It might've had something to do with the
sunshine and soft tropical breeze or the exotic food or even
the easygoing nature of the island's residents. Whatever it
was, she was thoroughly enjoying this assignment.

So far, she and her brother had attended a village fiesta,
complete with a whole-roasted pig at the center of the buffet
table. They'd hiked through jungle to see a remote waterfall
and donned a suit to walk the ocean floor. She'd loved it.

Blake would've loved it, too.

She quelled the sharp stab to her chest and stared through
the camera lens, her focus on the thousands of colorful foam
hearts inscribed with names and messages and dates. Cologne
had its Lock Bridge, and Guam had Two Lovers' Point, a cliff
line that towered over the northern end of breathtakingly
beautiful Tumon Bay.

It seemed fitting that tourists would want to leave a

symbol of love at one of the island's most visited attractions. It was, after all, a place where a centuries-old love was founded only to be tragically lost a short time later.

But what kind of parents insisted that their daughter marry for anything other than love? Or who'd disapprove of their daughter's choice because the guy wasn't some wealthy Spanish captain, but from a modest, local family instead? There was more to life than money. Zandra knew that better than most, and so far, leaving the security that money brought had been so freeing. Look at all she'd experienced since leaving the family business. First, an assignment that had taken her through three European countries and, now, a visit to a tropical paradise. She couldn't ask for much more. At least, that's what she told herself.

Zandra lowered the camera and adjusted the settings.

Well, one thing's for sure, no way would she allow anyone, especially her parents, to dictate who she should marry. She'd have taken the same route the young lovers did, tying their long hair together and jumping off the cliff rather than live a life that would have been nothing short of miserable.

"How's the shot?"

She smiled at her brother. It hadn't taken long to get into the rhythm of the photo shoot, with Jackson automatically making adjustments to each scene.

In much the same way Blake had.

And there was that stabbing feeling to her chest again, the kind that came each time she thought of him. It was as if her heart held out some false hope that things could be different between them, but it was impossible. They both knew it.

"Zandra?"

She blinked. Jackson had asked a question. What was it again? Oh, that's right... "The shot's fine." She swiped at the drop of sweat on her forehead, while the tourists who walked around them seemed immune to the tropical humidity. "I'll frame this one off-center, with part of the cliff jutting out."

It was the same section of cliff that local legend claimed represented the young female lover, her profile eternally etched in rock. She waved Jackson over and opened up her Instagram app. "I'm doing another IG live."

"Now? Weren't you just on it?"

She rolled her eyes. Another one who didn't understand the importance of social media. "Now. And, for the record, I haven't been on since last night at the village fiesta in Santa Rita. Besides, I have a few followers who said they set their notifications because they were excited to see a behind-the-scenes live."

Zandra walked away from the crowd, sucked in a deep breath, and practiced a smile. Bubbly and playful and fun— all the things she didn't feel at the moment but had to conjure up anyway. She could do this. Blake had taught her how, and she—

Ugh. Blake again.

Okay. Deep breath. She stared beyond the metal rails to the seemingly endless ocean beyond, the waters of the vast Pacific crashing onto the base of the cliff below. Behind her, tourists jostled for real estate along the wall, conversing in Asian languages and carrying selfie sticks like an important travel accessory.

It was just another day in paradise.

"You ready?" Jackson raised an eyebrow expectantly. "The sun's pretty bright, just so you know."

Ah, yes, his way of telling her to hurry up already. She blew out a deep breath and nodded. With a tap, she opened up the live feed and waited for the connection. She waved as the viewer count started to rise. "Hey there, everyone." Zandra spread an arm out and grinned. "Welcome to Guam. So this is my third day on the island, and it's been an absolute blast. Yesterday my brother and I hiked through the jungle to Talofofo Falls. I posted some pictures from it last night, and I'll link it to a story this afternoon so it'll be easier to find.

"Anyway, Talofofo Falls was gorgeous and definitely worth the trek."

She peered at the screen and the smattering of comments that scrolled up. "Hey, Tina." She grinned and waved at the screen. "Yes, I'm still alive. No, I haven't forgotten that you're getting married next weekend." She laughed. "I'll be there, so quit worrying already."

She panned the camera, keeping herself outside the shot as much as possible. "Isn't this place beautiful?" She paused, letting it capture the foam hearts. "The hearts are so cool, aren't they? You all know how much I love hearts."

The heart is the sign of life. While it beats, there is time to love, to laugh, to live. But you must do so quickly because you do not know how long it will continue to beat.

From the past, Jacques' words reached out to her and made her smile.

She scanned the questions once more. "No, the hearts are made out of foam so are quite light. Hey again, Natalie. I'm getting ready to shoot a cultural session with some of the island's local weavers a little later this afternoon. They'll be making bags, bowls, hats, and even jewelry all from coconut fronds. It's very cool!"

She peered closer at the screen and read off some of the questions. "A coconut frond is—"

Zandra blinked at her phone screen and the male figure behind her. What the... "Blake?"

She spun around to face him. "What are you doing here?"

"I had a few days leave, and I thought I'd pop in and see how you were doing."

"From *Japan*?"

He shrugged. "Why not? It's a short plane trip away."

The longing rolled in, as hard and fast as the waves a surfer would ride. She swallowed it down, tamped it as hard as she could...and failed miserably.

God, she'd missed him. Really missed him. But there was no reason to think his presence was anything more than a polite hello before he went off and did Blake things...was it?

"You're going to lose that thing over the cliff," Jackson said, reaching for her phone. "Hand it over."

Shock clearly took over as she handed her brother the phone. "What the hell's happening here?"

"Talk to Blake." Jackson turned and held the phone away from him. "Hey there. For those of you who don't know me, I'm Jackson, Zandra's older brother." He waved. "She's a bit indisposed at the moment."

"Zandra?"

She closed her eyes, savoring the melody Blake's voice created when it melded with the sounds of the lapping waves of the Pacific Ocean on the rocks below.

With a deep breath, she turned, still half wondering if she was imagining things. "Blake." He looked so damn good in a T-shirt and board shorts, it was all she could do to stop from hauling herself into his arms. She swallowed past the rapid thumping of her heart and fisted her hands to her sides.

"How did you find me?"

"Instagram." He held up his phone. "I opened an account and set my notifications. Last night you said you'd be at Two Lovers' Point, so here I am."

Zandra blinked. He'd opened an Instagram account? For Blake to do so was huge, but what did it mean? "So now you're stalking me?"

"No."

"Then what are you doing here?"

He pulled his sunglasses off and propped them onto his ball cap. "I brought you this," he said, holding out his hand.

There, in his palm, was a gold key encased in a vividly colorful swirled glass heart.

She stared, emotion welling up inside her, threatening to overtake her. "This was from Strasbourg," she whispered, taking the heart from him. It felt warm in her hand. More than that, it felt *right*.

"From the glass shop," he confirmed.

The world faded away until all she saw was Blake. He readjusted his ball cap, his gaze latched onto hers like he never intended to let go.

"I remember that place," she said slowly. The vulnerability and sincerity etched in his toffee-brown eyes took her breath away. "How…why… I didn't see you buy this when we were there."

"Well, I did."

He did. Obviously. Questions swirled through her brain much like the colors of the heart, but she chose to ask the most obvious one. "Why?"

Blake reached for her hands, the glass encased between their palms as shivers of electricity traced through her. "You see hearts wherever you look. And when you look at this, I want you to know that *you* are the key to *my* heart, to my future. I want you to know that, no matter what happens, no matter where we end up, my heart belongs to you."

God, she wanted to believe him, yet she still held back. "But we have to be realistic, Blake. We're on two different paths, and there's practically little hope we'd get to spend much time together. How're we supposed to make a relationship work?"

He squeezed her hand, the heart pressing into her palm as memories of their time in Europe flooded her brain. "So it'll be a long-distance one. So what? People do it all the time, and I know we'll figure it out."

His smile crossed the small gap between them and

chipped at the wall around her heart, but she still couldn't bare her heart to his. "Didn't you once say that you didn't want anything to screw with your path? Hate to break it to you, but a relationship would definitely do it."

He nodded, his gaze not leaving hers. "I thought it would, but then I realized that Jacques and Martine were right. Reaching for my future means that much more with the right person around to share it with. If I have that, there's no way my life *could* get messed up."

"And you're sure I'm the right person? Why?"

He seemed to consider that for a brief moment. "I love your optimism," he said. "Your sense of adventure...the way you focus on your work...how you never give up, even if it means countless lessons on how to read a train schedule."

"But I have opinions that don't always agree with yours," she pointed out.

"Which forces me to examine life from a different angle. This isn't a bad thing."

"What about law school? You're still going to law school, aren't you? Because there's no way I'm letting you leave your dreams behind."

"I'm still going to law school." He squeezed her hands again. "It'll work out. It'll all work out. With you in my life, how could it not?"

Could he mean it? Could he really want her in his life? "I'm not giving up my photography career."

"I'd never ask you to do that." He shook his head. "Capturing the essence of who people are, of what it's in their soul, that's your superpower. It's who you are. I'd never want you to walk away from that."

"You'd better accept it," Jackson said. "At least, if your followers have anything to say about it, you will. And Tina thinks you need to bring him to the wedding."

"Wait?" Zandra whipped her head toward her brother.

"Are we still live?"

"Yeah." He held out the phone. "And they're all saying you should accept his apology and keep him." He made a face. "For the record, there are some things a guy shouldn't know about his sister and his best friend, so wrap it up already."

"I love you." Blake stepped toward her, riveting her attention to the preciousness of this moment. "I always will. So what do you say, Zandra version 2.0? Do you think you'd be okay with someone sharing a crazy life adventure with you?"

Her heart broke free, opening up so that love and hope flowed through her, the emotion so beautiful she was sure it would rival the Pacific Ocean beside them.

Blake was here. With her. He wanted her. He loved her.

Her heart felt full, overflowing with love for this man, this moment, and the moments yet to be. She loved him. And she couldn't wait to live a life with him in it. "There's only one logical answer," she said, squeezing his hand this time.

"And that is?"

"Yes."

Epilogue

The auditorium was packed with graduates and guests, and while Blake typically hated crowds, he'd waited years to be a part of this one.

"Get ready," he said. "Mom's class is up next."

Beside him, Zandra held her camera up. "I'm a go. My new lens should make for perfect shots from up here."

"Don't pay any attention to him," his sister Lily said as she leaned across him. "I swear he acts like he's the one graduating."

"Right?" Zandra chuckled. "He's been kind of nervous about all this."

"Hey, I have a lot riding on this, too," he said, grinning.

Zandra captured his gaze. "I know." She raised a hand and stroked his cheek. "You'll be up there getting *your* diploma before long."

His smile broadened, and he rubbed his hands together. "Yeah." And he couldn't wait.

But all things happened in their own time.

In the two years since he'd taken a chance and flown

to Guam, Zandra had traveled the world, sometimes able to incorporate her assignments with a visit to where he was posted. It hadn't been easy, but they'd found a way to make their non-traditional relationship work despite the distance and time zones between them.

It'd been worth it, though. Her photographs had earned her recognition, and Blake couldn't be prouder. Watching Zandra pursue her dream only made him more determined to pursue his.

"Constance Monroe."

His mother's name rang through the auditorium, and Blake stood and whistled, clapping his hands alongside his sister. True to her word, their mother looked in their section and waved.

"Got it," Zandra said, lowering the camera and scrolling through the shots. "I think there's some good ones in there."

"No doubt," Lily said. She opened her purse and grabbed her keys. "I'll head to the apartment and get the food ready for Mom's grad party."

"We'll be over as soon as we can get her to leave," he told her.

Blake looked at the floor of graduates, a swell of pride coursing through him. There. It was done. Everything his mother had worked toward all these years summed up in a walk to retrieve a piece of paper. She was on her way...and now it was his turn.

He leaned toward Zandra as other graduates were called to receive their diplomas. "You know," he began, his stomach a collection of nerves, "I've decided to leave the Army in a couple of months, just as I'd planned."

"Yeah, you've mentioned that," she said, scrolling through her camera gallery.

"Well, I have something very important to ask you." Nerves or not, he had to dive in and do it.

"What's that?"

"I love that you're doing what you want because I wouldn't want it any other way. But I wondered...would you move in with me? I know you'll be gone a lot, but I figured that maybe I could be your home base." His mouth dried, and his heart hammered like it was determined to beat out of his chest. He sucked in a deep breath and tried to calm the hell down.

Zandra stopped, set her camera on her lap, then turned to face him. She blinked as if processing what she'd heard, then her face formed into the smile that Blake would never tire of seeing. "Because I love you, I have to give you the only logical answer to that question."

"And that is?" he prompted.

"Yes."

"Well, okay then." He sucked in a deep breath and grinned, and his heart finally settled, slowed to a pace where he knew he was at peace. Yeah, it was the most logical answer all right. And that's when he also knew the best was yet to come.

Acknowledgments

I am so thankful for the many talented people who pulled together to take this book from a kernel of an idea to a story ready to be shared with the world.

Lily, I cannot thank you enough for playing tour guide and traipsing through Europe with me while I did the research for this book. You're the best travel partner ever, and the fact I couldn't figure out the train schedule wasn't your fault! LOL. Lord knows you did your best. Maybe we should go back so I can try again?"

Fred and LovieAnn, Del and Lil, thank you all so much for answering my endless Army questions and not rolling your eyes. (You didn't, did you?) Any incorrect military references in this book are mine and are probably because I wasn't listening carefully enough, didn't take good notes…or there was too much bourbon flowing!

Nadine Mutas, thank you for helping with the German translation. Your input was very much appreciated, my friend!

My incredible critique partner, Meredith Clark, I thank you for keeping me on the mostly straight and sometimes narrow and for asking such stellar questions like, "Now why is the hero like that?" and not taking "because" for an answer! Next time I decide to write without filling out my plotting board, please remember to bitch-slap me. Seriously.

To all the CrossFit coaches who keep me sane, particularly Andrew, Ethan, Ken, and Colin, thank you for letting me sneak in a quick workout when I'm on deadline! Some days writing is like a chipper, and I think of you all pushing me to keep going even when I don't want to. (Kinda like when you program 400m runs into a WOD!)

Heather Howland (a.k.a. Editor Lady), you keep it real, pull no punches, and always push me to be a better writer, even when goats are involved! Thank you for believing in me and sprinkling your editing magic on this book. I'm really glad you're my editor!

To the team at Entangled Publishing, I am so grateful for your patience and hard work. Thanks to you, Blake and Zandra are out in the world!

About the Author

A native of Guam, Melia Alexander is the author of sassy, sexy, fun contemporary romances. She's fortunate to work at The Male Observation Lab (a.k.a. her day job at a construction company), where she's able to observe guys in their natural habitat. She likes to read, catalogue her shoe and handbag collection, and search out the perfect sunset, preferably with a glass of cabernet sauvignon and a box of dark chocolates. In an attempt to balance out her life, she also attempts to conquer her CrossFit fears: ring dips, power cleans, and the dreaded 800-meter run. Stay in touch with Melia on Facebook, Instagram, and her newsletter.

Find love in unexpected places with these satisfying Lovestruck reads...

THE BEST FRIEND PROBLEM
a *Mile High Happiness* novel by Mariah Ankenman

All that's missing from Pru's life is a baby. Luckily, it's the twenty-first century—she can take matters into her own hands. Until Pru goes in for a fertility check-up to find…she's already pregnant. With her best friend's baby. As best friends, Pru and Finn have survived college, new jobs, and bad breakups, but can they survive crib shopping, birth classes, and late-night cravings? Especially when Finn has never considered himself even remotely Daddy material?

THE ARMY RANGER'S SURPRISE
a *Men of At Ease Ranch* novel by Donna Michaels

Army brat Kaydee Wagner's grandfather needs help repairing his home, so she steps up. She has no clue what she's doing, but surely she can wing it? Wrong. Help arrives in the form of troubled former Army Ranger Leo Reed. After a very…*wet* incident involving deadly dance moves and a wayward sink hose, their clothes hit the floor faster than a stack of tile. Leo doesn't want forever. Kaydee only wants right now. Their white-hot attraction should be the perfect arrangement…until hearts get involved and Kaydee discovers she's pregnant.

TROUBLE NEXT DOOR
a novel by Stefanie London

McKenna Prescott is the queen of picking the wrong men. When her latest boyfriend dumps her, she decides to devote her time to "exploring herself" (read: drinking wine and ordering sex toys online) and starting her freelance makeup business. That is, until an embarrassing delivery mix-up puts her sexy, gruff neighbor in her path...

HER SEXY CHALLENGE
a *Firefighters of Station 1* novel by Sarah Ballance

Caitlin Tyler doesn't do bridges. Cue the cocky, infuriating fireman who goads her off the bridge. He's hot, but he's also exactly the kind of guy she wants to avoid...which she manages to do for a whole four hours. Lt. Shane Hendricks is only two weeks away from leaving Dry Rock. He sure as hell doesn't need to get involved with a woman he has to rescue twice in one day. They're moving in different directions. Leaving should be easy, but falling for Caitlin might be the one fire he can't put out...

Made in the USA
Monee, IL
03 March 2025